Carved in Stone

MORE PHANTOM ELEMENTS

The Water Ghost
Out of the Fire
Carved in Stone
Air Asylum

October 2018

PHANTOM ELEMENTS

Carved in Stone

Jennifer Campbell

Big Blue Press

OKLAHOMA

www.phantomelements.com

No part of this publication may be reproduced or transmitted in any form, without written permission of the publisher. Big Blue Press is an imprint of ChromaStory Books.

All Phantom Elements books are works of fiction. Names, characters, places, or incidents are either the products of the author's imagination or are used fictitiously. Any resemblance to any persons, living or dead, any businesses, or locations is entirely coincidental.

Big Blue Press books are available for special discounts when purchased in quantity for educational use or fundraising. Find more information at www.chromastorybooks.com or www.phantomelements.com.

ISBN: 978-0-9982452-2-5

12 11 10 9 8 7 6 5 4 3 2 1   15 16 17 18 19 20/0

Text copyright © 2017 by Jennifer Campbell
All rights reserved. Published by Big Blue Press

Printed in the U.S.A.
FIRST PRINTING, 2017. BIG BLUE PRESS

PZ7
.C1615
Ca
2017

For Micah and Noah. Because of you both,
I know what true love really looks like.

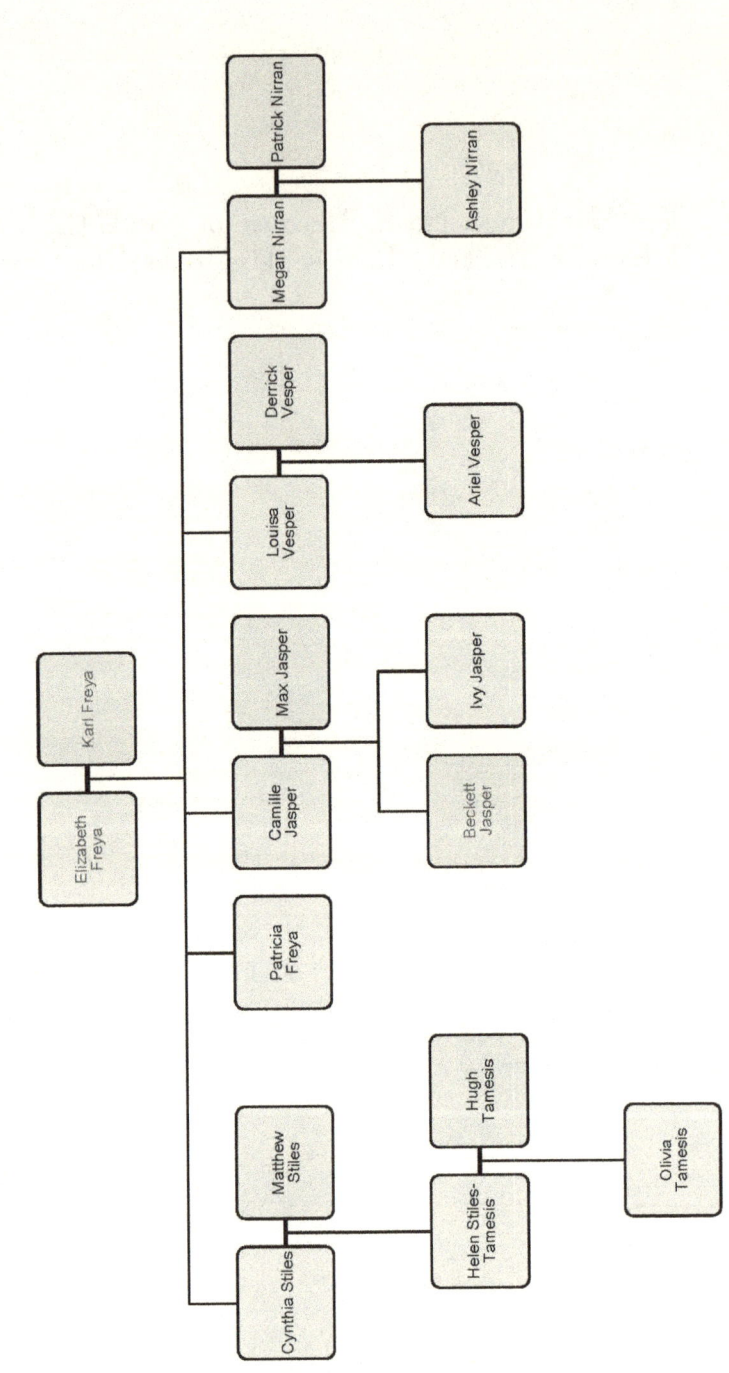

CHAPTER ONE

If You See Her

Onyx hiked through the forest, feeling the air fill his lungs, the last of the fall leaves crunching under his feet. The sunlight pilfered through the trees. The particles of light clinging to the forest floor seemed to rest for a moment, before they were sucked away into the gray underbrush. The air was clear and the only sound was the whistle of a bird calling, but going unanswered.

The voices of his friends had faded away. They were clowning on the rocks at Big Cabin Pointe, but Onyx had slipped away. He felt trapped, constricted, and sometimes he just needed to escape.

Last year, just after his fifteenth birthday, he started growing so quickly, he wasn't sure if there would be an end, or if he would end up a giant. He stretched his arms out, shaking out his biceps. He felt like he could never find enough space.

He was always hungry. His mom was a great cook and fixed large family meals, but it seemed like he could never eat enough. He would wake up in the middle of the night, his stomach gnawing with hunger. Tiffany Rainwater had begun to leave her son a plate of leftovers in the fridge with a note attached. Love you son, hope this helps.

Onyx knew his mom wanted to help. She had tried everything to ease his aching limbs: creams, ice packs, heating pads, but nothing helped. He heard her whispering to his dad at night.

"Jay, we have to do something."

His dad was almost seven feet tall. He knew there was nothing his mom could do or his dad could say to ease the aches or stave off the hunger.

His feet flew over the leaves, the rocky carpet of the forest. He leaped over boulders and fallen logs. He turned around a small, mossy cliff. His signature black sneakers flew over a narrow creek and past one of the jagged boulders carved with the strange markings.

The boundary stones were placed throughout the forest. Some said the Stone Witch had placed them around the Gray King's land. The old legend kept most people away from this part of the forest, but Onyx never minded. This was the only peaceful place where he could stretch out and feel the pain in his limbs melt away.

Everyone knew about the runestone in Heavener, Oklahoma. A large boulder, carved with Norse runes, drew visitors from around the world every summer. Historians and experts came to study the runes. A professor from Oxford determined the party had sailed up the Mississippi River and settled in the area. They were led by the Gray King, Harek of Inksgate. Some said he had married a witch, a sorceress who could control the winds and the waves, allowing him to sail across the great ocean to the New World.

Along with the stones placed throughout the forest, were stone statues of men, Viking warriors with iron age weaponry. Scientists had tried to carbon date them, but their results were always inconclusive. What's more, the statues seemed to be hollow. Some said the Stone Witch carved them herself, with old magic, but no one knew why, or what they meant.

The forest was a drop in a large nature reserve, a national park, meant to preserve the land and animals from the Oklahoma drilling and oil pipelines. Families across the state enjoyed the waterfalls and caverns of the area. Everyone said the hiking trails and natural springs did wonders for the body and soul, but no one dared to go into this part of the forest. They said bad things happened to anyone who crossed into the Gray King's land. Hikers had gone missing and strange quakes shook the ground. The Stone Men, the statues placed around the boundary, seemed to move on their own. No one could explain it so most people stayed away, but Onyx never had a reason to stay away. He had grown up exploring the land with his dad, Jay Rainwater, who was the head ranger at the park. He never felt uneasy.

Not until today. There was no sign of rain on the radar. The sky was clear, but the whole forest floor was wet. This must be the creek bed drying up, Onyx reasoned with himself.

Some said the Stone Witch could control the weather. Everyone in Big Cabin had their own ideas. No one had ever seen her, but they said if you did, you could never leave the forest. If you meet her, you're sentenced to life in the forest. If you see her, she'll turn you to stone.

If you see her, you belong to her.

Onyx's shoes began to slip over the slick surface of the creek bed that ran through the forest, like a vein through some dark creature that lay sleeping under the gray sky. A sharp crack cut through the silence. Onyx slowed his pace as his heart began to pound.

He was sure he wasn't being followed. No one would dare to go this deep into the Gray King's forest. He couldn't even call for help, since he didn't get cell service this deep into the wooded land. That was the allure.

These days, his cell phone seemed to buzz nonstop. He felt sick just thinking about it. The vibrations in his pocket sent waves of nausea through his entire body, but out here, he could just be alone with his thoughts. His body felt at ease, loose and free.

A swish of tattered black fabric sent his

head twisting backward. His feet skid across the wet rocks in the center of the creek bed. The trees hung over the stream of rocks, filtering out the sun. Onyx froze.

A light haze covered the ground. The temperature dropped. Another swish of fabric flowed through the trees. All the chambers of his heart began to hammer in his chest. He turned on his toes and bolted for the east, toward Big Cabin Pointe, but in one instant, he felt his feet swing out from under him. He fell, crumpled toward the rock-ribbed ground, catching himself on his shoulder. Stabbing pains shot through his right arm, followed by the burning sensation and metallic scent that told him he was bleeding.

A wisp of the black cloak swept over him. Onyx's black eyes dilated up into the canopy of the forest as a hooded form bent over him.

If you see her.

Red ragged waves of hair spilled from the hood of the cloaked figure. Onyx was frozen. He tried to move his body, but couldn't. The bright green eyes peered into him as if she were looking for something. Her eyes were framed by long lashes. Her lips were deep purple, like a dark bruise and they parted as if she were trying to say something.

Onyx took in a wracked breath. The pale skin of her face was marred by deep black lines, swirling into a haphazard pattern over her nose and cheeks. Her forehead was marked with the same ink in short lines. He wondered of she had done that to herself. Onyx was mortally terrified.

The Stone Witch drug an unnaturally long finger through the wound on his arm. She held the blood up to the light, peering through the single red drop that fell to the rocks below.

"What do you want?" Onyx croaked out in a strained voice.

The Stone Witch waved a cloaked hand over his face, and then, everything went black.

CHAPTER 2

AT REST

Ivy swept her hands under her round sunglasses. Her head seemed foggy, her thoughts pulsating behind her eyes. She crossed and uncrossed her legs, picking at a thread on her cut off shorts.

"She'll be okay." Her dad, Max Jasper, turned to her smiling but hiding tired eyes of his own behind Persol sunglasses.

"When?" Ivy asked, setting her *cafe au lait* in the saucer, rattling the spoon and sugar cube wrappers. "When will she be okay?"

The herbalist's shoppe was in a small alley behind the *Rue St. Jaques*. Ivy's mom, Camille, was receiving a treatment to restore the minerals back into her bones. Apparently, conjuring pounds of gold at the whims of your older sister took it out of you.

"I don't know, Ivy Pie," Max shook his head.

They sat outside a cafe, across the street from a large public garden in Paris. The *Jardin des*

Tuileries was in full bloom. Butterflies flitted from flower to flower.

I guess they can just take what they want and fly around without a care in the world, Ivy thought. The bitterness crept up like bile in her throat. Who in their right mind is jealous of butterflies?

Ivy took a sip of the robust, frothy brew in her cup and chewed on a croissant. Everyone raves about the croissants in Paris. Ivy had eaten the same thing every morning while her mom was at the herbal treatments. She had come to equate flaky pastry, milky sweet coffee, and fresh clementine juice with waiting, anxiety, helplessness, and frustration.

"I'm worried, too," her dad admitted, his own breakfast going untouched.

"Why us?" Ivy crossed her arms over her plaid shirt. "Why mom? Why Beckett? Why can't I just be normal and go to a normal school again? Have a normal life?"

Ivy thought back to her old school in Phoenix. They had moved from Denver to Phoenix when Ivy was nine years old, just months after her brother was killed. Beckett Jasper was sixteen years old and had been playing baseball with some friends. He was struck by lightning. In Denver, she was the girl who's brother had been in the accident. People either walked on eggshells or avoided her. When they moved to Phoenix, everyone knew about her brother, but it seemed as though they forgot that they knew and started treating Ivy like every other kid.

"Ivy, what happened to your brother," her dad began, pulling off ribbons of the croissant and shredding them for the pigeons, "that was an accident."

"Mom just got pushed into conjuring a metal that depletes all the minerals in your body, almost killing her," Ivy finished what she thought was her dad's thought.

"It was her choice," Max concluded, pushing back his sandy blonde hair.

"You know she always does what Aunt Patricia wants," Ivy said, the frustration flaring. "And don't get me started on Aunt Megan. I guess they finally had to tell her when Ashley started showing the signs."

Patricia Freya, and three of her sisters, Cynthia Stiles, Louisa Vesper, and Ivy's mom, Camille Jasper had decided to hide the family magic from their youngest sister, Megan. With only four elements, they had wrongly assumed that Megan would be skipped. Patricia's magic was powered by fire, Cynthia's by water, Camille's by the earth, and Louisa's by the air.

The girls practiced their magic under their mother, Elizabeth Freya, not thinking that Megan would manifest any powers. Yet, when Megan turned thirteen, she began to exhibit her very own special blend of plant magic. Twenty years went by with Megan doing nothing more than blending plant oils. Her powers were weak, so everyone in the family was shocked when Megan's daughter, Ashley, began to exhibit incredibly powerful fire magic. Patricia moved them close to her home in Tulsa and months later they called Camille with a request for two kilograms, almost a pound of gold.

"You got yourself into trouble with the Alchemists?" Camille had shouted. "How could you? Don't you know what they're capable of? And Ashley is messing around with one of them? I can't believe you let this happen."

"You should be glad we found out. This affects all of us," Patricia lectured.

Three months later, Patricia, Megan, and Ashley had wasted thousands of dollars on unnecessary repairs on their downtown storefronts. They had lost the trail of Price Phillips, a high ranking official in the Order of the Alchemists. All the surveillance on their family had disappeared. Ashley was marked forever with cursed iron. Blaze Hathaway was too stupid to know what he could do to Ashley with her own feelings for him. Maybe he really did love Ashley, but it didn't matter. It wouldn't take long before the other Alchemists figured out that they had direct access to Ashley Nirran, because Blaze would come back for her.

Ivy's blood had boiled when she saw it in the crystals. The quartz pillar she was staring into cracked right down the center.

The breeze moved through the garden

stealing the scent of lilac. Her mother would be a few more hours at her treatment.

"Let's go do something fun," her dad said, sitting up straight in the wicker cafe chair.

Ivy sighed. She had planned to meet Laur, the waiter, at the *tabac* and let him buy her French candy and cigarettes. She was fourteen and he was seventeen, that wasn't so big of a difference, was it? Besides, the French did know how to kiss.

"Okay," she conceded with a small smile and an eye roll. Laur would wait for her. They always waited.

The air turned noticeably cooler as Ivy and Max Jasper descended the iron steps into the Catacombs. Ivy's feet buzzed on the iron. She was getting tired.

"Almost there," her dad whispered.

"I don't know about you, but the Catacombs weren't my first thought when you said 'fun'".

"Okay, peaceful," Max corrected.

Ivy nodded. Her head had been buzzing since they came to Paris. They roamed all over to try to find a place for her mom to rest and heal. Paris sat on a limestone quarry, hollowed out and used at one time to house the city's dead. What resulted was the Catacombs, a macabre but beautiful display of the bones of the forgotten citizens of Paris.

The limestone seemed to be restorative to Camille, so the Jasper family rested, hidden in the city until Camille was strong enough to go back to the States. Ivy knew which state they would end up in. She was desperate to avoid Oklahoma and the rest of her mother's sisters. Patricia seemed to be drawing them to her and Ivy was wary of her intentions.

The cool air traveled over Ivy's skin, relaxing her. Her dad was right. The Catacombs were beautiful and peaceful. In a bittersweet moment, Ivy let her thoughts travel to Beckett. Her brother was vibrant, as if light spilled from every pore. He never sat still. He would jog backward while talking to you. He would hide to scare you but then feel guilty about it and back out at the last minute.

"Ivy, I'm in the kitchen with a squirt gun!"

He would still chase her until she found the garden hose, but at least he was always honest with her.

Part of her hoped he was at rest, and part of her hoped he was her guardian angel. Maybe it was a little mix of both.

"Ready to go?" her dad asked after they had strolled through the sculptures of skulls and bones.

Ivy nodded.

She padded over the limestone in white sneakers, careful not to disturb the quiet. As she walked out of the Catacombs, Ivy stopped. She was sure she had heard something, but when she turned around, nothing was there. She turned back around to face the sunlight streaming in from the top of the exit. She looked up, but if she had looked below, she would have noticed the skull, now petrified limestone, turn to look at her and then swivel back into its final resting place.

CHAPTER 3

JADED

"We're not going back, Mom. We came to Paris for you to heal and rest," Ivy pleaded.

Conjuring the gold to save the downtown storefronts had left Camille sick and weak. Camille used all of her strength to cast the spell and her reserves were critically depleted. That's the thing with magic. There's always a price.

Speaking of, Price Phillips, the mayor who was secretly a member of a society called The Alchemists, dedicated to hunting witches and either exploiting their magic or eradicating them completely, was sitting safely in prison. The thought did little to comfort Ivy. For every rat you see, there are fifty you don't. His daughter, Kylie Phillips was on the run and would undoubtedly team up with her uncles, Wade and Lincoln Phillips, and her older brother, Zach Phillips, who was away at Dartmouth studying biochemical engineering.

Cynthia Stiles had done her homework via

a private detective agency and had shared everything she knew with her daughter and sisters.

The counter surveillance had revealed murmurs of The Alchemists growing and spreading across the country. Ivy shuddered to think of what they would do if they were ever able to get their hands on a real, live witch.

"The Alchemists are hunting us, Ivy. They'll find us, wherever we are. There's no hiding," Camille insisted. "Patricia needs us."

Patricia didn't need them. Patricia, Megan, and her spoiled, know-it-all daughter, Ashley needed an endless supply of money to fuel their half-baked magic and fund their mistakes. Ivy didn't care if she saw them ever again.

Last year, Ivy's cousin, Ashley had a major run in with a nasty entity known as a shadow phantom. She was able to banish it to the spirit realm, but she had no idea what spell she used, and she hadn't been able to recreate it since.

There was no doubt in Ivy's mind that Ashley was a powerful witch, but she had no idea how to control it. She thought she was being careful. Ivy could see Ashley when she gazed into the amethyst crystal at her bedside. Her cousin hadn't set up any protective spells or enchantments and she left herself defenseless to Kylie.

Ivy sighed.

What's worse, Megan Nirran, Ashley's mom, Patricia and Camille's youngest sister, was still new to her own magic. Moving to Oklahoma and being surrounded by Patricia Freya and Cynthia Stiles, their oldest sister, had activated the family magic, powering Megan's dormant plant magic and Ashley's uncontrollable fire magic. Patricia thought Ashley was a fire witch like her, and she may be, but Camille had taught Ivy early on that all witches have their own Element Signatures and no one was exactly alike.

Cynthia thought that her youngest sister Megan had simply been skipped, like her daughter, Helen Stiles-Tamesis. Helen had been blessed with a high intellect and striking beauty, but still remained unable to conjure any magic. Still Helen was a scholar and with some luck and her daughter Olivia's emerging water magic, she was able to uncover the lost poems of Angelina Fontanez, a mysterious and reclusive poet. Helen revealed to Camille that Angelina's poems may be more than what they seem.

"You're still too weak to travel," Ivy insisted.

Ivy rested her hand on her mom's thin wrist. Camille smiled and closed her eyes. She was covered with patches soaked in an herbal potion.

"Only a few more hours," the tiny woman croaked in her ancient voice.

The Healer lived in a small apartment on the top floor of a building on the *Rue Poncelet* in Paris. Ivy wondered how she got up and down the stairs. Maybe she didn't have to, Ivy mused. Healers were some of the oldest and most revered beings in The Light. Most witches lived in isolation, afraid of their powers, but if they were lucky, they found their way to The Light. The loose network of magical beings stretched across the globe and took every precaution to stay hidden and underground.

Ivy smiled and nodded her thanks. Last week she had stood Laur up. Most nights she met him under the canopy of his cafe at sunset and walked with him down to the Seine, talking and smoking.

"That's bad for you," he said in his thick French accent.

He was tall and thin and had one crooked tooth that crossed over slightly onto one of his front teeth, but he was handsome and came with an endless supply of French cigarettes and day old baguettes.

"I know," Ivy sighed.

Even though she was only fourteen, Ivy had been smoking American Spirits with the hipsters in downtown Phoenix for two years. She went out most nights with her best friend, Everly. Her parents, then geologists, were too depressed by Beckett's death to care. They had thrown themselves into their work, not looking up.

Everly was willowy with shiny blonde hair, and always gathered attention wherever she went. Ivy was shorter, with curvier hips and dirty blonde hair. Ivy's hair was darker, her skin was tanner, and her green eyes were green where Everly's were blue. It seemed as though she were permanently walking around in Everly's shadow.

"What?" Everly had fumed when she found out that Ivy was leaving Phoenix.

Ivy hadn't wanted to tell her. She knew it would be one of Everly's massive blow ups. Most people shied away from Everly's temper, but Ivy didn't mind. If she was in the shadows it meant there was less chance of anyone finding out her secret.

She was lost in thought that night when Laur had taken two of his fingers, made a peace sign, and pushed the corners of Ivy's mouth up.

"Smile, American," he laughed.

She shook him off. It was supposed to make her smile, but she just looked like one of those mimes. They went back to smoking and kissing, sitting on the barriers to the river while the limestone pulsed beneath Ivy's body.

"You don't have to sit with me, honey," her mom's voice floated to her.

She was so light and frail. Ivy was afraid if she hugged her mom, she might break. Every time she looked at her once vibrant mother's pale gray skin, and hollow cheekbones, she could feel the anger rise in her stomach. She knew she was just drowning her senses with Laur, trying to rid herself of the gnawing resentment, but at the time it made sense to her.

"Don't worry about me so much, Ivy Jade,"

Camille whispered, tilting her head back to rest on the chaise in The Healer's apartment.

    Ivy gave her mom's hand one last squeeze. She descended the steps to the small courtyard and out onto the street. The ancient cobblestones scuffed at her white sneakers. She dug her hands into the pockets of her cutoffs and headed for the smoke curling up from the familiar red cafe awning. In two hours she would be back at the Seine with Laur and in two weeks she would be back in Oklahoma with her family. She couldn't help but feel more jaded and bitter than ever.

CHAPTER 4

TO SHREDS
SCOTLAND, 1128 A.D.

The fires swirled in the night outside the small hut that Morgana shared with her mother. Iona shouted out to the laird that Morgana was innocent. Morgana knew she wasn't. Yesterday, the laird's eldest son, Tiernan MacNagaulla saw her in the meadow behind their hut.

Tiernan had always followed her around the grounds. When she turned eighteen, Tiernan and his father, the laird Forlan MacNagaulla had insisted that Morgana and her mother, Iona move into Castle Dirleton on the shore. Iona's husband had been killed building one of Forlan's massive warships and she wasn't about to hand over her only daughter to the laird and his oily son, but still Tiernan would not be halted in his pursuit of Morgana.

"Your daughter is the devil's bride and she will be punished," Forlan's deep voice boomed throughout the hollow, almost shaking the small hut.

Morgana had been collecting herbs around their hut that morning, when a tree branch snapped at the trunk and came crashing down on her leg, shattering the bone in her upper thigh. She cried out, and Tiernan, who had been lurking around under the guise of hunting boar conveniently heard her cries. Morgana thought she was alone, so in her agony, she sailed the hefty tree branch off her leg and into the forest. Her skin and hands glowed as she healed her own broken bone. Tiernan had watched, spellbound.

"I gave you a chance, witch," Tiernan bellowed.

In his defense, he had given her a chance, stroking his red beard. The choice was simple. She could marry him and live in the castle, using her magic to kill Forlan, thus giving Tiernan the lairdship he so desperately wanted, or undergo the witch's trial. She would be thrown into the sea, at the mercy of the ocean. If she were a good Christian woman and not a witch, God would spare her life. If she were a witch, she would drown, but not before undergoing Tiernan's special brand of torture.

"The world will know what you are," Tiernan cried as he drove an axe into the front door of their tiny stone hut.

Morgana and Iona struggled to move the

baskets of potatoes off the door to a secret passageway, leading to a meadow beside the hut.

"It's going to be okay, my bonnie darling," Iona swept a hand over Morgana's cheek.

Morgana's rich red curls were drenched in sweat, her green eyes wide with terror. Tiernan's axe splintered through the dry wood. A mud caked boot kicked in what was left of the door.

"Laird Forlan, please! Tiernan, please show mercy," Iona begged.

"Please, Tiernan!" Morgana echoed her mother's pleas.

Tiernan rose the axe and drove it down into her mother's chest. Blood instantly coated the axe as her mother's ivory face went blank. She crumbled to the dirt floor of the hut.

"Mama," Morgana wailed. She tried to go to her mother's body, surrounded in a growing pool of blood. The deep wound in her chest poured out, saturating her mother's gown a deep crimson.

"Wrap the body and bring me the girl," Tiernan ordered.

Forlan's men took over and drug Morgana out of the hut. They tied her to one of the horses and drug her to the castle, the dirt path peeling off most of the skin on her legs on the way. She was nearly delirious with blood loss and pain by the time they made it to the castle courtyard.

When the horses stopped, Morgana had the chance to breathe. The ropes were made of plants. She fought through the pain and focused on the ropes. She exhaled a thin breath over them. One of the soldiers took a step back as the ropes turned to dust.

"Laird Forlan! Master Tiernan!" he shouted.

Morgana took two steps back looking for an exit, but her injured legs failed her and she collapsed to the ground.

"Get the chains," Tiernan shouted.

The men grabbed her once more and wrapped her in iron chains. They sizzled when they touched her skin, seeping the power out of her body. All she could do was sob as the pain tore through her.

"You will be judged for your sins," Forlan boomed, as Tiernan wrapped her in more chains and bound her to a stake in the castle yard.

"You could have been queen," Tiernan said, under his breath.

"I'd rather die," Morgana hissed.

"That can be arranged," Tiernan laughed.

Tiernan shoved her head against a wooden post in the courtyard. He nailed one side of a leather strap to the spike and fixed the strap over her forehead. Morgana struggled in her chains, but grew weaker by the second. Tiernan produced a small knife from his pocket.

"Now, I'm going to make sure you are marked for all eternity. You will never go to heaven. You will go straight to the depths of hell where you belong," Tiernan said.

"Nothing like a lass scorned," Morgana

said, managing a small sneer, right before she spit directly into the beard Tiernan spent hours oiling in his vanity.

Tiernan growled and sunk the knife into her face. Morgana screamed as Tiernan carved the knife through the flesh of her cheek, stopping to slam her jaw shut to carve lines into the other side.

Sharp breaths tore through her chest, rattling her teeth. Her eyes were wide with terror and hate. Tiernan stopped to swipe the blood off on her bare shoulder. Part of her cloak had been torn off, dragging her to the castle.

Tiernan drove the knife back into Morgana's face, this time, cutting small gashes into her forehead above her eyebrows, and slicing a curved swipe down her nose. Her forehead strained against the leather strap, but she couldn't move.

Tiernan scooped up a handful of ashes from the large fire pit in the center of the courtyard. He grabbed Morgana's heart shaped face in his gloved hand. She coughed as she breathed in the ashes.

"The world will know," Tiernan snarled and smeared the ashes into the open cuts on Morgana's face.

She screamed a choking peal of terror as the ashes marked her skin and then passed out in agony, slumped against the stake.

Morgana woke to sunlight and the gentle

rocking of waves. A searing pain bit into her face. She was lying on the deck of the MacNagaulla warship. Her chains were gone. The wood pulsed with life beneath her and her limbs tingled and ached, like stretching out a tight muscle. Her legs had healed already from being drug to the castle. Morgana could feel strength growing back into her bones.

Next to her, a body wrapped in cloth lied unceremoniously on the deck. A large red stain bled through the wrappings on the chest. Her mother.

A few moments after blinking into the sun, she felt a sharp yank on the top of her head. A rough hand pulled her head up. Tiernan's foul breath crept up her neck. The cuts on her forehead tore open again as he pulled her hair back. The spray of the salty ocean sent stabbing needles of pain through her entire face.

"Just look at you," Tiernan sneered.

He threw her forward to hang her head over the side of the ship.

Morgana was able to see her face in the water's reflection. Lines swirled around her cheeks, red from the blood and black from the ash rubbed into the open wounds.

Morgana's hot anger broiled to the surface. The wood of the ship began to crack under her feet. She held back. Something told her to wait. She knew she was more powerful now than ever, but she needed to wait just a little while longer.

"Throw that one overboard and gather the men for the trial," Forlan instructed.

Two men grabbed Iona's body and tossed her into the sea. Morgana was roughly pushed forward onto the lower deck of the ship. The wood groaned and popped. Forlan's men looked at each other nervously. Forlan ignored the ominous sounds and continued on with the trial.

"Morgana, daughter of Riordan and Iona, you have been charged with witchcraft. How do you plead?"

Morgana remained silent. She would confess to her crime, and much more.

"Guilty," she said after a long beat of silence.

Forlan and Tiernan looked at each other.

"You would deny yourself the witch's trial and the possibility of the laird's mercy?" Tiernan asked.

"I am guilty of having powers, Tiernan," Morgana said.

She felt her fingers elongate. Her arms grew and snaked toward the mast of the ship. Her skin grew cold like smooth marble.

"I am guilty of conspiring with you to kill your father," Morgana shot a glare at Forlan.

The shock registered on the old man's face that his son had conspired to cut his life short to usurp his lairdship.

"I am guilty of killing you and all of your men," she shouted as one of her fingers snaked around the closest warrior's neck, snapping it in two. The lines on her face illuminated as her skin reacted to the ashes. "And I am guilty of destroying your finest warship."

The color drained out of Tiernan's face as Morgana levitated before him, her face lined and scarred, and her arms snaking out of her gown. Her fingers grew snakelike and wrapped around the entire warship, gripping it like a child's toy. The ocean floor rumbled, churning the waves and tossing the boat. Sea water poured over the walls of the ship. Morgana still gripped the sides of the ship with the tentacle-like appendages she had grown from where her arms once were.

"If I am to die, you will all die with me," she cast. "May the ocean have mercy on you, Tiernan."

A thousand sickening cracks permeated the air as the massive warship splintered and ripped apart, torn to shreds by the witch, still levitating over the sea. Morgana watched as Forlan and Tiernan struggled and then disappeared below the churning surface. When she was satisfied with her work, she collapsed and allowed herself to be taken over by the sea, tossed along with the waves, at one with the ocean itself.

CHAPTER 5

ALL STAR

"Aiden, come on!"

Dylan was yelling at the top of his lungs for Aiden Franks to run after the pop fly hit to right field. It was only the first game of the single elimination state tournament. All star teams from around Oklahoma had converged on the Dunn rec park that weekend for the massive tournament that would end the season. Those like Onyx who played football as well, could start football camp the following week. Others could play fall ball in the wooden bat leagues or start target practice for bow hunting season. Some would rodeo, but some would resume their time spent in other ways.

"You can surf the couch later, Aiden! Come on!"

Dylan threw his catcher's mask down in the dirt and kicked at home plate.

"You better watch it!" the umpire called, slicing through the air with a stern finger.

"Aw, that's bullcrap!" Dylan yelled back, not

wanting to swear and get ejected from the game altogether.

"I'm warning you, son!"

"I got it! I got it!"

Aiden came jogging back up with the ball in one hand, panting and smiling. It didn't seem to matter to him that all three runners already crossed home plate. Mono had swept through Prue, taking out four of their players so Aiden was called up.

The center fielder had made his way to right, trying to help Aiden, but he waved him off.

"This is my big moment! Let me get close enough to throw it in. I got it!"

"Your mom's got it, Aiden!" Dylan yelled on his way back behind home plate. Coach Howard just shook his head and spit a spray of sunflower seeds across the dugout floor. Dylan had been pretty cranky ever since his break up with Brooklynn. To make matters worse, Sadie Lee was renewed with a sense of passion about making Dylan her boyfriend, but he was not interested in the slightest.

"She came over to my house and didn't even take off her shoes. Do you know how many germs there are in just your driveway alone?"

All the guys had a pretty good laugh about that one at the expense of Sadie Lee's massive collection of high heels and Dylan's germaphobia.

"It's okay Dylan! We still love yeewwww!" a shrill voice rang out from the stands.

Dylan mumbled something under his breath and kicked at the dirt. If the umpire had heard that string of expletives, Dylan would be kicked out for sure.

Onyx leaned back in Big Cabin's dugout, laughing to himself. It had been a pretty easy day. Caleb was pitching and Flip was at shortstop, so between Caleb's wicked curveball and Flip stopping everything at short, he'd had a pretty big snoozefest in left field. Normally he played first base, but they had picked up Caleb's cousin and wanted to try him out at first on Prue. Since the mono epidemic, they were down four good players. No big, Onyx would just cruise in left and have plenty of time to hang out with Harbor, the other team's star player. They had met at baseball camp last year and had become pretty good friends.

Big Cabin's next batter popped one up and Dylan caught it, making three outs after a very long and tense bottom of the fifth.

Mercifully, the innings switched. The Big Cabin Bulldogs were up eight to nothing on the Prue Warriors as Onyx trotted out to left. Harbor stepped up to bat. He was good but he got nervous trying to hit off Caleb.

"Go Harbor! You can do it!"

A pretty, dark haired girl cheered him on from the stands. Onyx recognized her from Facebook as Olivia, Harbor's girlfriend of almost two years. The annoying girl in the stands with pounds of makeup melting off her face practically sneered at Olivia. What was that chick's problem?

Olivia was sitting with two other girls and a guy. The taller girl looked like Olivia, with full lips and high cheekbones, but she had pale ivory skin and auburn hair. She was holding hands with the guy with neat, dark hair and tan skin. He looked athletic, but not bulky. A soccer player maybe? Track? It wouldn't kill that guy to crack a smile, Onyx thought.

The other girl sitting by Olivia was shorter, with long, dark blonde hair. Onyx couldn't really see her, she was sitting behind one of the backstop posts, but he could make out her shiny, waist length hair. It turned a reddish shade of gold in the sunlight. She stood up to move around and Onyx could make out her distinct style, frayed cutoffs, a slouchy tank top with another lacy tank underneath, a thin choker necklace, round sunglasses, and she had an amazing golden tan. Her skin was almost the same color as her hair. She had the same full lips as Olivia, but a shorter, adorable button nose. Wow.

"Onyx! We are playing baseball!"

Onyx heard the crack of the bat about two seconds too late. Harbor's pop fly sailed over his head and dropped a good five feet behind him.

Well, crap.

Onyx had to scramble. He was sure he looked like a dork in front of the girl he was checking out, but he was able to hold Harbor off at third with a triple. Maybe that was the strategy, have Olivia bring her gorgeous friend to distract the other team.

Onyx looked up to the stands a few minutes later. Olivia was still there, but the other girl was gone. Maybe she wasn't even real, Onyx thought. That would make twice this week that he had seen a ghost.

The next day, after Big Cabin had won the whole tournament, Onyx stayed with Harbor and his family at one of the big lodges along the lake. The Talbot family rented out the eight bedroom lodge with a few other families, and they were going to spend a week out on the lake, fishing, tubing, and wake boarding.

That afternoon, Onyx, his best friend Flip, Harbor, his best friend Kai, and Dom, the uptight kid with the dark, gelled hair cruised around the lake on Harbor's boat.

One of Flip's favorite raps came on the boat's speakers and he started dancing. Flip did not have a chill bone in his lanky body. Fernando Dominguez had earned the nickname "Flip" when Onyx once showed him a magic trick in the sixth grade. Flip was new to school and Onyx tried to make him feel welcome with a trick he did for his little sister. He made a quarter disappear under a cup. Flip jumped up on his chair.

"Nah, man! How did you do that?"

Flip had been flipping out ever since then.

Did your mom bake cookies? Flip stuffed two in his mouth, ran around the school and made her one thank you card per week for five weeks straight. Did you get an F on a test? Flip tore the test to shreds, made picket signs and learned to play the trombone for a protest march against the unfair test. Is Big Cabin going to state? Yes they are, so Flip learns to repel and jumps from the gym ceiling, repelling into the pep rally like something out of Mission Impossible.

Now he was shaking Kai by the shoulders, shouting, this is the best song ever!

Onyx tuned them out and stared off into the distance behind the boat, watching the lake churn up a frothy wake. He had no idea what to make of the ghostly woman in the forest. He hit his head when he was hiking and when he woke up, he was alone in the bottom of the creek bed. Did he imagine it?

Onyx sucked in a breath. If anyone would understand, it would be these guys. They've all had run-ins with the paranormal. Two years ago, Harbor and Olivia found Harbor's grandpa's buried gold and lost poems from a famous poet by following clues left for them by the poet Angelina's ghost. The mysterious Water Ghost, Angelina Fontanez, had been haunting the lake for decades but now, seemed to be at rest.

Dom was just talking to Harbor about the fiery shadow phantom that haunted a building around their downtown storefronts. Dom was saying that Ashley had banished the phantom with a spell and that Olivia may have the same magic as Ashley. Dom and Harbor thought Olivia may have helped find the gold using powers she didn't know she possessed.

Onyx decided to wait until Flip was wake boarding and take a chance. He waited until the perfect time and then told the guys everything that happened and what he had seen in the forest.

"What?" Onyx asked when he was finished spilling his guts. "You guys think I'm crazy?"

"No man, it's just, your face is really white," Harbor said.

"You look like you've seen a ghost," Dom quipped.

"I know what I saw," Onyx said.

"Trust me man," Harbor laughed, elbowing Dom in the ribs. "We'd be the ones to believe you. Weird junk follows our girls around, so we do know somebody who can help you."

"It doesn't freak you out?" Onyx asked.

"Nah dude, just a day in the life," Harbor smiled.

"And she's worth it," Dom added, glancing at Ashley waving to him from the shore.

Olivia and Ashley had arrived with the beautiful blonde girl from the ball park. She had different funky shades on and part of her hair was tied into a knot. Onyx felt himself start to sweat in spite of the cool spray of water off the lake.

Harbor waved and smiled to the girls and they all waved. Olivia and Ashley smiled back.

"Olivia's cousin Ivy's being cranky today, I see," Harbor surmised. "We'll check in with them later and see if they have a solution to your, what did you say? Your Stone Witch problem."

Ivy.

Onyx shook his head. If the family resemblance and the frown on Ivy's face were any indication, he was in big, big trouble.

Okay, All Star, Onyx thought to himself. You've never backed down from a challenge. Let's do this.

CHAPTER 6

Over The River and Through the Woods

"Camille! Come in here!"

Cynthia's outstretched hands engulfed her younger sister. They had all seen each other at Harbor's Freedom Tournament yesterday, but they still embraced warmly, getting used to being close again.

"Louisa?" Camille asked, her eyes hopeful.

"No, I'm afraid not," Cynthia said.

Ivy gazed behind her Aunt Cynthia up into the Victorian home nestled into the rocky cliffs by the lake. Cynthia Stiles had bought the home on Keystone Lake in the Shady Grove area, just across the large lake from Hugh, Helen, and Olivia. Everyone almost fell over when Hugh Tamesis, the law professor, announced that he was buying a boat, so the Stiles-Tamesis family could visit each other without having to drive.

"At least he'll have a reason to wear all those dorky boat shoes," Olivia had said.

Cynthia, a powerful water witch, could now manipulate the water levels the way she turned on a faucet, so the Tamesis family could finally have the boat at their dock. Ivy and her parents had driven in. They couldn't see the water from the front of the house, but looking out to Cynthia's dock would have revealed Hugh's new boat, as well as a visitor from down the lake.

"You have a friend here, Cynthia," Camille smiled.

They could all hear each other telepathically, but Ivy was having trouble with that. Cynthia smiled. Her silvery white hair glinted in the sunlight.

"A friend," she said.

Ashley and Patricia were in the back by the lake, practicing their fireworks. It was the Fourth of July, the one day when they could make fire, sparkling flares, and huge booming firebombs without raising an eyebrow. Helen and Megan were in Cynthia's large kitchen, cooking up a feast. Helen may have been passed over with her mother's water magic, but she was still a wizard in the kitchen and Megan knew just what to do with the fresh vegetables she grew in her rooftop garden, an oasis resting on top of their downtown storefront.

Olivia stood waiting with Cynthia outside, hanging back. She made a small wave to her cousin, Ivy.

"Hey," she managed, when Cynthia had spoken her greetings and ushered everyone inside.

"Hey," Ivy nodded back. "How did Harbor's game end up?"

"They got beat pretty bad. Big Cabin is really good," Olivia nodded.

"It looked like it," Ivy said.

Everyone except that cute left fielder. He looked athletic, but he couldn't make a play to save his life. Maybe that's why they stuck him in left field.

"I bet this is pretty weird, huh?" Olivia asked with a small shrug.

"No, not really. I've been doing magic since I was little," Ivy said, rolling her eyes.

"I mean us being all together."

"Oh," Ivy said, taken aback.

Now that she thought about it, it was a little weird. The Freya sisters had been scattered across the country for so long, and now, they were back in their home state with their daughters cruising around the same lake they swam in as girls. It was strange for Ivy to spend time with her family she had only heard about just days before.

Olivia stubbed the toe of her Converse sneaker into the gravel of the driveway.

"Yeah, it's a little weird," Ivy admitted.

"Ashley's out back," Olivia said.

"I figured, with the fireworks," Ivy said.

"They're not doing any magic tonight," Olivia chirped. "We're all going to watch real fireworks over the lake at Appalachia Bay. Harbor and his friends are taking us."

"Do they have cars?" Ivy asked.

Olivia's boyfriend just turned sixteen, but Harbor and all of their friends drove the backroads on their permits anyhow. Still, Ivy would rather be with a licensed driver after being scarred forever with Paris traffic.

"No, on their boats."

Even better.

"It should be fun?"

Olivia sounded hopeful. Maybe Ivy should back off and give her a break.

"Okay, sounds cool," Ivy admitted with a smile.

They went inside to help Megan and Helen put the feast out on the back table. They had whipped up spicy deviled eggs, sticky Dr. Pepper ribs, baked beans, cool pineapple slaw, bacon potato salad, a creamy fruit medley, and jalapeño cornbread. Everyone hauled the serving platters into the long, ornate Victorian dining room as fast as they could so they could get started.

Olivia and Ivy filled their plates and nestled onto the steps of the gilded staircase, balancing their plates on their knees. Ivy realized she was famished and sunk her teeth into a meaty rib.

"Your mom is an amazing cook," Ivy said. "Are you sure she doesn't have any magic?"

"Nothing powered by the elements," Olivia admitted, chewing a mouthful of sweet, smoky baked beans. "Grandma Cynthia thinks she got skipped."

"I forget that Aunt Cynthia is actually your grandma. Does that make me your aunt?" Ivy asked. "It's kind of confusing. Somebody should keep a family tree or something."

"She has one," Olivia replied. "It's up there."

Olivia shot her eyes up the stairs to the second floor landing. Ivy wondered why Cynthia wanted this big Victorian house. Sure, it was beautiful, but it had to be a boat load of work, no pun intended.

"She has one and The Alchemists have one," Olivia trailed off.

"The Light doesn't keep them. The Seer knows everything," Ivy said.

"What's The Light? And who is The Seer?" Olivia asked.

"No one told you?" Ivy asked, taking a buttery bite of cornbread.

Ivy started to explain about The Light. When her mom was in Paris, they had gone to a Healer, who was part of The Light, a network of magical beings dedicated to helping and preserving their kind. The thing was, you would only be able to locate The Light if you were in need. Ivy was beginning to tell Olivia about the Healer when a flash of bright auburn hair whipped around the banister.

"I am so hungry! You guys are already eating? Is everyone eating?"

Ashley Nirran.

"You can only do so much," Ivy quipped with a sharp, ironic smile.

"I just have to practice," Ashley smiled. "You can't get better if you don't practice. Aunt Patricia has been so cool to help me. I did the most amazing spell a few months ago. I banished Prospero Phillips' shadow phantom to the spirit realm. It was incredible. Did your mom tell you?"

Ashley stood at the end of the staircase, in front of the doorway with her hands on her hips. She was wearing soccer shorts and a "Don't Hate the 918" t-shirt.

"Like my shirt? I should get you one since you live here now. It's the area code, get it?"

Ashley's long muscular legs were silhouetted in the sunlight and her hair floated around her face in red strands. She looked like fire come to life.

"Oh, hi. Nice to see you today," Ivy said flatly.

Ashley spent the whole baseball game talking to Domino the other day, and had barely said two words to Ivy. Now she wanted to talk?

"Oh-kaaay," Ashley smiled a wide smile with gritted teeth. "Well, I better go get some food. Aunt P is going to try to show me how to make lightning."

"Lightning? I'm not hungry anymore," Ivy stated as she stood up. She felt heavy, like stone. "I think I'm going to be sick."

"Ivy," Olivia cajoled.

"I'm gonna step outside for some air," Ivy said, dumping her plate into a large trashcan.

Ashley glanced to Olivia, who was shaking her head, pressing her lips together in a frown.

"What? What did I say?" Ashley said, looking bewildered.

"Her brother-" Olivia whispered.

"Oh god, I didn't mean-"

Ivy stepped outside.

The air outside was fresh and light. Ivy sucked in a full, greedy breath. She didn't know how to process Ashley. She was glad Ashley had fought off the shadow phantom in the museum, but no one knew how she did it. She exposed Price Phillips as an alchemist but had left his daughter, Kylie, to escape with all the research on their family. Their coven. That's what was happening. Cynthia was calling her coven together in the most twisted version of "to grandmother's house we go" around.

Before she could think too much, the crunch of aluminum made her jump five feet.

"What in the balls!"

"Sorry," a voice like sandpaper chuckled behind her. "Didn't mean to scare you."

Ivy turned around to see an older man in a navy polo, pressed olive slacks, and what looked like a veteran's hat. He had been in the Army, it seemed.

"Were you in the Army?" Ivy asked.

"I was," the man answered.

Ivy grabbed his arm. She shook it slightly and then poked him in the shoulder.

"Whoa there, sister. What are you doing?"

"Checking to see if you're real. I've seen ghosts."

The man laughed.

"Well, I'm not dead, yet."

He threw the beer can in the trash.

"Are you my Aunt Cynthia's friend?" Ivy asked.

"You don't look like you've seen a ghost. You look like you've seen the enemy," the man said. "You're too red in the face to have seen a ghost."

"My cousin's just," Ivy made a face, "-ugh. So, how do you know my aunt?"

"Whoa, good thing it's a barbecue 'cause you sure do know how to grill."

Ivy sat with her hands folded. The man laughed and raised his bushy eyebrows.

"Well, alright, yes, I'm Cynthia's friend. Dwight."

"Did you ever fight in a war?" Ivy asked.

"Yep, Vietnam," the man answered.

Ivy nodded.

"We learned in school that a lot of people protested the Vietnam War. Lots of people didn't think we should be fighting."

"Well, that may be so, but when I came

home, the hippie girls were excited to see me," Dwight laughed. "If you know what I mean."

Dwight earned himself a blank stare in return for the joke.

"Did you believe in what you were fighting for?" Ivy asked.

She didn't mean to be rude. She knew it was a heavy question, but she had to know. She was losing her mom. Her mother's bones were being depleted from the inside out. She was losing a battle in a war she didn't want to fight.

"Well, I can tell you one thing for sure, doll. You may think you know what you believe in, and you may think you know what you're fighting for. You may think you're fighting for freedom, or your country, but when you're there, when you're in the battle, on the front, you're fighting for the ones closest to you. When you're at war, your fellow soldiers are your brothers, and in battle, you're fighting for your family."

Ivy nodded.

"Ivy!" Olivia's voice came through the patio door. "Did you still want to go watch the fireworks?"

Ivy hesitated for a second then grabbed a Coors Light from the cooler next to Dwight. Gross, she thought, examining the label and tossed it to Dwight.

"Thanks for the advice," Ivy said.

"You weren't going to take that, were you?" Dwight asked.

"You have a crush on my aunt, so you wouldn't have told," Ivy shrugged.

"Could have used a pistol like you in Vietnam," Dwight called after her.

Could have, Ivy thought. If he had Cynthia Stiles with him, he could have drowned the whole enemy army in a matter of minutes, but that was beside the point.

CHAPTER 7

NO IDEA

The poor guy had no idea, Ivy thought to herself. She half floated, half skidded down the rocks behind Cynthia's house to where Harbor's mom was going to pick them up.

"Can't do that, can you?"

Ivy tossed back the thinly veiled insult to Ashley, who was crunching down the rocky trail behind the back patio.

"What is your problem?" Ashley asked, the frustration huffing out of her voice. "Look I'm sorry about your brother, but-"

"You didn't even know him! You think you know everything," Ivy snapped. "You think that just because you had a few magic lessons that you're a super witch or something."

"I didn't say that!" Ashley screeched.

A thin film of golden flame washed over Ashley's body. Ivy could feel the frustration rolling off her.

"You think you're all powerful and you act

like you don't need other witches," Ivy said, shaking her head. "But you still make my mom supply you with gold at the drop of a hat. Do you have any idea how long she was sick? Do you?"

"A year ago I didn't know there were any other witches. Give me a break! We were going to lose our homes, Ivy," Ashley said.

She sounded like she was talking to a child. Even though Ivy was only a year younger than she was, the placation oozed out of Ashley's voice.

"Cynthia has a big enough place. Why don't you just move in with her?" Ivy asked.

"You just have it all figured out, don't you?" Ashley asked. "Dom was going to lose his family's restaurant. My friends were going to lose everything."

"And your family?" Ivy shot back. "I could have lost my mom!"

"That was her choice!" Ashley screamed. "That was Aunt Camille's choice to help us."

"She had zero choice. You and Aunt Patricia gave her no choice and you know it!"

"Oh really," Ashley said, with a massive eye roll powered by sarcasm and ire. "We were just supposed to let Price Phillips, the leader of the Alchemists, run us out of town and burn up Blaze and Dom in the process?"

"Blaze first, huh?" Ivy snapped.

"That isn't fair," Ashley practically growled.

Ivy's anger was burning hot. A small

rumbling shook the ground. The air crackled with static electricity.

"Would both of you control yourselves?" Olivia hissed. "Someone could be watching."

"And you?" Ashley turned to Olivia. "What do you even know about magic? You refuse to use your water magic, or even help us."

Olivia sighed. The roar of a boat engine in the distance made her turn around. A boat sliced through the water.

"You both just need to chill," Olivia ordered.

It was clear that she wasn't messing around. She didn't want their cover to be blown.

"Olivia!" Allison Talbot, Harbor's mom was at the helm. Her hair was tucked up into a baseball cap and her silver aviator sunglasses reflected the three girls standing on the dock, Olivia in the middle of her two cousins.

"You girls have to come on, if you're comin'!" Allison shouted. "Ashley, I have to take you to Domino and then you two have to go. His mom is having the baby!"

Ashley gasped. She let out a small yelp. The girls climbed into the boat and Allison sped off across the lake to where Harbor, Dom, and the guys were hanging around, fishing with the pontoon boat. Allison Talbot had taken the fastest boat to get to Ashley. She had a feeling Dom's little sister wasn't going to wait very long.

Ivy hadn't looked at Ashley since they stepped onto the boat. She was turned around, looking behind the boat at the wake, but when she shot a glance at Ashley, she noticed her rubbing a spot on her palm. She must be nervous for Dom, for his mom.

"Do they know if it's a boy or a girl?" Ivy asked, trying to break the ice wall between them.

"A girl," Ashley smiled. "Veya. Veya Chavez."

When the boat rolled into the nearest dock, Ashley hopped off and ran around to the other side of the small peninsula in the middle of the lake. Ivy, Olivia, and Allison followed. Ashley caught Dom's attention and waved wildly. Apparently his cell phone was dead the whole time his mom, Ignacia Chavez, had been trying to call him. Everyone was on their way to St. Francis to welcome the new baby, who decided to make her arrival three weeks before her due date.

Ivy folded her arms and frowned. She's concerned about everyone's family but her own, Ivy thought bitterly to herself. Olivia walked up behind Ivy on the dock. She put her arm around Ivy's shoulders. Ivy felt her muscles relax and her breathing slow.

"Fire witches just run hot," Olivia said. "And stone witches are, well, a little-"

Ivy nodded.

Olivia didn't need to say any more.

Dom and Ashley sped off to Harbor's house where Ashley's parents, her Aunt Patricia, and Dom's Uncle Ernesto were waiting for them. Ivy was glad to see Ashley go, but she felt guilty. She didn't want to fight with her family, especially when they may need each other. They may be each other's last line of defense to protect their kind.

"Come on," Olivia stretched her hand out to Ivy. "Let's relax and have some fun tonight."

Olivia guided Ivy onto the pontoon boat where Harbor and his friends were waiting to take them cruising around and to see the fireworks that night.

"Are you sure you're not using any of your element at all?" Ivy asked.

She knew water witches could manipulate moods and feelings. Ivy was slowly becoming aware of the calm replacing the bubble of anger and frustration in her stomach.

"I have no idea what you're talking about," Olivia smirked. "Now come on, let's go see some fireworks."

Ivy nodded and grabbed the cheap sunglasses she had bought on the street in Paris to shade her eyes from the setting sun, but immediately pulled them down when she saw the guy on the boat from the baseball game.

He was crazy tall and wearing black board shorts with a gray and black striped tank top. Acrylic clear and black sunglasses perched on top of his inky black hair and tanned face. He turned and smiled a row of white teeth, with one of his eye teeth jutting out slightly to the side. His eyes were a dark charcoal gray with black spiky irises splaying out from his pupils. He had a pink bracelet on his thick wrist, with a princess charm dangling to the side.

"Ivy, you know Harbor from the game, and this is Onyx, his friend from Big Cabin," Olivia introduced Ivy to the kids on the boat. "And this is Kai, and Onyx's friend, Flip, and Aiden, and Grace."

Olivia's voice trailed off. Kai offered Olivia his hand to help board the boat. She took it and smiled her thanks. Kai was still staring after her and waved to Harbor as Olivia made her way to the front of the boat.

Onyx was still looking at her. Maybe it was Olivia's calming presence or maybe it was the new town. Maybe it was the fact that she had left her old self back in Paris or that Everly's toxic voice in her head had almost disappeared. The voice that said, no way, that guy would never be interested in you. You're too short, too squatty, not thin enough, not pretty enough, too chubby. That voice was almost gone. If it was Olivia's water power, or if it was her own strength coming back, she had no idea. She was just glad the doubt in herself was slowly, but certainly disappearing.

Onyx's phone rang. He put one finger up to let everyone know he'd be back.

Ivy moved around to the back of the boat to secretly listen in on the conversation.

"Uh huh," he said, his voice softening. "I'll be home in a couple of days. I miss you, too."

I knew it. He has a girlfriend, Ivy thought to herself.

"Well, Mom told you to stop wiggling it. It'll come out when it's ready, Bay. The tooth fairy won't come if you yank it out and spray blood all over the house."

Or maybe he has a sister and I'm an idiot, came her next thought. The bracelet. Duh.

"Okay, well, just go eat an apple and see what happens."

Onyx was pacing the back of the boat, his full attention focused on the girl at the end of the line. It made Ivy's heart ache for Beckett.

"I don't know Sis, try a red one and then a green one. No, a peach won't work. It has to be crunchy. I swear, they're not gonna let you in the third grade, Bailey."

Ivy smiled.

"Okay, I love you. Bye."

His voice is so deep and he loves his sister. I have no idea what I'm going to do, the thoughts went bouncing around Ivy's head. Say something cool.

"Hi," Ivy said, lamely raising one shoulder. "Nice bracelet."

"Oh, thanks," he returned with a wide smile. "It's Aurora, the princess from Sleeping Beauty. She's Bailey's favorite. Bailey's my sister. She would really like your hair."

Ivy smiled. She felt cool and confident, but strangely relaxed. She turned to Olivia at the other end of the boat. Harbor was driving and Olivia was leaning against his side. She gave Ivy a strange smile and turned back to the front, leaving Ivy alone with her new friend.

CHAPTER 8

Strange and Complicated

Onyx cringed. *My sister would love your hair.* That was the first sentence he had uttered to the most gorgeous girl he had ever dropped a baseball for. Onyx thought Olivia was pretty when he first met her, but her cousin was a knockout. She looked like hitting a home run feels. Unexpected, but amazing.

"Nice to meet you," Onyx said, sticking his hand out after suddenly remembering his manners.

"A handshake?" Ivy asked.

She shook her head with a small, cute smile.

"Yeah, we're not meant for handshakes," Onyx admitted and wrapped Ivy up in a hug.

Ivy laughed and took a step back. She jutted one hip out.

"And what if I wanted a high five instead?" she laughed.

"Sorry?" Onyx said, widening his grin.

Ivy just laughed. Harbor made a motion

to Onyx from the front of the boat, the international symbol for "come here." Onyx shook his head. Dude, no, not right now. Harbor motioned with a little more vigor and then picked up the boat's loud speaker which had formerly been playing Little Big Town.

"On the Pontoon," Aiden sang along off key and wiggled his wide backside.

"Onyx Rainwater, would you please move to the front of the boat at this time," Harbor's scratchy voice came through the speaker.

"Aw, turn it back on," Aiden commanded. "Makin' waves and catchin' rays and get some food."

"That's not how it goes, babe," Grace giggled.

Aiden pointed at her and made another little shimmy with his shoulders.

"Jumpin' off the back, don't act like you don't want to."

"Harbor, what?"

Onyx had to dance around Aiden's freak show he had going on to get to the front of the boat. This better be good.

"That's who can help you, you know, with your problem," Harbor said.

Harbor was so proud of himself. Onyx wanted to punch some sense into him. He wasn't about to tell Ivy about the ghost witch in the forest and the stone men who looked like they could come alive and kill him within seconds.

When Harbor said he knew someone who could help, Onyx thought he was talking about Olivia's grandma or something, not her cousin, who was even more stunning than Olivia herself, by the way.

"No way, bro. I can't tell her that. She'll think I'm weird. We just met. I have to ask her stuff, like what's your favorite movie, you know, crap like that."

"Says who?" Harbor asked. "I told Olivia all about Shep's ghost when I first met her."

"He did," Olivia confirmed.

"No."

Onyx pulled Harbor's t-shirt up over his head so he couldn't see and shook it a few times for good measure.

"Bully! We're gonna crash! Olivia, take the wheel, please!"

"Drama queen," Olivia said, laughing.

The boat was out in the middle of the lake. They weren't in any sort of danger, but they were going to miss out on the fireworks if they didn't get going. Onyx grabbed two Sprites out of the cooler and headed to the back of the boat.

"Go in peace, man! Namaste," Harbor called after him.

"What were you guys talking about up there?" Ivy asked.

Onyx shrugged. He tried looking cool, but seconds later, he admitted defeat and breathed out a heavy sigh. He might as well try being honest if anything was going to work out between him and Ivy. When he had asked Harbor about her, Harbor said that she was fourteen and going to be a freshman in Heavener next year. That was perfect because Onyx went to Big Cabin, which was right next to Heavener in southeast Oklahoma.

"Okay, this is going to sound a little strange, but I know you're related to Olivia, so Harbor said you might be able to understand. So, here goes."

Onyx told Ivy everything, well, almost everything. He told her about hiking in the forest on Big Cabin Reserve. He told her about tagging along with his dad, a park ranger, whenever he patrolled the reserve. He painted a picture of the woods, the ravines, the waterfalls, and the thermal pools, his love for the land coming out in every word.

Ivy smiled, listening to him talk.

"It sounds awesome," she said in her twinkling voice.

"Well, here's where it starts to get a little weird."

Onyx explained that the runestone in the park was thought to have been carved by Vikings sailing up the Mississippi River. Scientists had determined that the markings were Norse runes over 1,000 years old. There were also several stones marking the area around the forest with the same runes. Cryptologists had determined that the runes were directional, meaning that they marked a boundary of some sort.

More recently, they determined that the runes spoke of Harek of Inksgate, named the Gray King. He was a fierce war king, raiding the coast of what is now Great Britain and many believe he stumbled on a supply of timber which allowed him to build the biggest fleet of raiding longships the world had ever seen, so he was able to sail across the Great Sea and travel up into North America.

"I know. My parents are going to start working, studying the runestone. I just can't believe there were Vikings around here," Ivy said, her green eyes glowing.

"Yeah, according to the experts like your parents that hang around the runestone. They sailed up the Mississippi and settled in the area."

Onyx was glad she was intrigued and not jumping off the boat and swimming for shore. Other girls would have run away, screaming. Onyx's phone buzzed in his pocket. He ignored it. It was past Bailey's bedtime, so there was only one other person it would be.

"But that's not really strange," Ivy said, making a face.

"Well, here's where it gets interesting," Onyx said.

He explained the myth of Harek's wife and queen, the Stone Witch. Onyx thought he saw Ivy frown a little, but she returned to normal soon enough so he kept on with his story. He told her about the Stone Witch and how she supposedly haunted the most interior part of the forest, the part where the trees filter out the sun.

"I've been there lots," Onyx admitted, "and I've never seen anything strange. Until I did."

Onyx paused and told her about the Stone Witch, with her shredded rags of a gown, her tattered hair, her sad eyes, and the horrid, dark marks cut into her pale face. He told her about seeing her face for a few haunting seconds before passing out.

"Are you okay?" Ivy asked.

Her voice was full of concern. At least her first question wasn't are you insane? Onyx was thankful for that.

"I can take you there and show you when you get back to Heavener. Big Cabin is so close. We can see each other all the time."

Tell her, a guilty voice gnawed in his stomach. Onyx pushed it down. They were almost to the shore and besides, they were just talking. What was the harm in that?

Harbor and Kai got out and docked the boat just as the sun dipped below the horizon. Onyx helped them unload and they moved the party to the small beach inside one of the coves at Appalachia Bay.

"Are you going to tell her?" Flip asked when he caught Onyx alone, unloading beach blankets.

"What do you mean?" Onyx replied, his voice hitting a high note at the end of the question. He cleared his throat and returned to a deep voice. "I mean, what do you mean, Flip?"

"You're catching major feelings, man. It's dark and I can see that with my shades on, bro. Ivy's tight. She's a cool chick but you need to tell-"

"I need to end things with Madison is what I need to do," Onyx admitted.

"Oh man! I knew this was coming!" Flip jumped up and down in his bright orange bathing suit. He was like a human signal flare. "I knew that was done when she was talkin' like 'Onyx do this' and 'Onyx do that.' You don't ever let a chick work you like that, bro. What you need to tell Madison is, look baby, it was real cool for a while, but you and me is-"

"Flip, okay. Okay. I got it. I'm cool."

Flip was still walking with his nonexistent butt sticking up in the air, impersonating Madison Vine, sophomore class president at Big Cabin High School.

"Knock it off," Onyx growled.

"I'm cool, man. Mind yourself," Flip said as he brushed himself off.

"Flip is so funny," Ivy giggled, walking up.

She was blissfully unaware of the conversation that just transpired.

Yeah, funny right off a cliff, Onyx thought.

He had been meaning to break up with Madison since Thanksgiving when she made a scene about being a vegetarian at his grandmother's house on Thanksgiving, but somehow, Onyx had just never gotten around to it. He knew his mom didn't like her either.

It was always something, though. After Thanksgiving came the holidays, then Valentine's Day, then homecoming, and before Onyx knew it, the school year was over. He didn't want to hurt her feelings. He had tried to break up with her a few times before, but she wasn't having any of that, so Onyx just let it be. He figured he was alright, just feeling numb for a little while until he figured things out. That was until he caught a glimpse of Ivy Jasper and made the first error of his whole entire baseball career.

Onyx promised himself that he would fix the whole Madison mess as soon as he got home and make things right for Ivy so he could be the boyfriend she deserved.

"It's a little cold on the water," Onyx smiled, shrugging off his hoodie and wrapping it around Ivy.

The fireworks glinted off her blonde hair, shiny bursts of red, green, and blue. Onyx had his back to them, but he could still see them reflected in her hair and her bright green eyes. Once he saw them reflected off of her, he didn't need to see the fireworks any other way. She looked magical.

"Aren't you gonna watch the fireworks?" Ivy asked with a shy laugh.

She had been eating a popsicle and her lips were stained red. Onyx couldn't help himself. He leaned in to kiss her.

"Your lips are cold."

Ivy wrapped her arms around his neck and kissed him back, cradling his face in her hands.

"Your hands are cold, too."

"Stop it!" Ivy laughed, landing a soft whack to his arm with the sleeve of his own hoodie.

Onyx laughed and pulled up the sleeve of his hoodie, revealing her soft hand. He held it in his and continued to watch the fireworks in her eyes. The bursts of light seemed to continue long after the sky had grown dark, and the sinking, gnawing feeling in the pit of his stomach had set back in.

Onyx needed to tell her, but he couldn't. It was complicated.

CHAPTER 9

Lindsfarne Priory on Holy Island, 1129 A.D.

Morgana jerked her head to the side, blinking into the blinding sun. Her face throbbed, but the searing pain had dulled to a slow ache. Panic raced through her. She held her hands up to the sunlight. Her limbs had returned to normal. Her hands were now just rough from the sand and saltwater.

"How am I still alive?"

"By the grace of the Lord, I suppose," a voice answered.

Morgana screamed and backed up on the shore, her feet tearing at the sand. She didn't realize she had said that out loud.

"I'm sorry, I didn't mean to startle you," the man said, his voice soft and benign.

"Who are you?"

Morgana spat out the question as an accusation. Yet, the man remained gentle.

"I am Father Thomas. You've washed up on the shore of Lindsfarne Priory. This is Holy Island."

Morgana laughed a laugh of pure hysteria. She held her head in her hands, and within seconds she was weeping. Her tears were so prolific that she was able to use them to wash away the sand on her hands.

The man was speaking Latin. Old Nan from Castle Direlton had taught her to speak little bits of Latin when she was a girl. It was their secret language until the old bookkeeper had died. Since it was clear that the man wasn't going to kill her, she laid her throbbing head back down on the sand. Father Thomas peered over her, amazed.

"Why is your face marked so?" he asked. "Are all women marked in this way?"

"What?" Morgana asked in disbelief.

Tiernan had said she would be marked as the devil's bride forever. Did this holy man know nothing of the devil?

"No," Morgana answered, and then stopped. "Wait, have you never seen a woman?"

Father Thomas smiled sheepishly.

"No, I'm afraid that in all my twenty five years, I have not," he admitted. "There are women in the village nearby, but I have never left the grounds."

"What about your mother?"

The word stabbed daggers through Morgana's heart. Visions of Tiernan driving an axe into her mother sent hot anger spreading throughout her chest.

"She left me on the steps of the priory when I was a babe. I have no memory of her," Father Thomas confessed. "The monks took pity on me."

"Have you never been to the village?" Morgana asked.

"No," Father Thomas answered. "There is no need for me to go. And your face, all women do not have these markings in your land?"

"No, they do not," Morgana answered.

She sighed and told Father Thomas the truth. She had already faced death once, and everyone she loved was gone, so she figured honesty would at least be the best course to safety. If she was found out to be anyone else, her lies could get her killed.

She told him about growing the herbs, Tiernan's attack, and her dark scars from the ash he had rubbed into her face. She confessed about tearing the warship apart and drowning Forlan's crew. She told him her heart's truth, that she wanted Tiernan and Forlan to die. She wanted them to pay for what they did to her mother. Perhaps Thomas would see her for what she was, and end her life as the devil witch she was.

"You can grow herbs?" he asked in awe. "What else can you do?"

"Did you not hear me? I said-"

"I heard your confession. Believe me, I have heard worse. God will forgive your sins if you pray for forgiveness. You will receive His grace and mercy. Now, show me, can you grow elderberry? Horse chestnut? Garlic? Lavender?"

Morgana nodded. She dragged her hand through the sand and turned up rich, fertile soil. His eyes widened. Within seconds, tiny sprouts formed in the dirt. They grew, sprouting new leaves along the way, forming thick vines twisting in the small patch of soil and finally blossoming with fruit and flowers. Thomas stood back, amazed.

"You are an angel," he whispered, tears forming at the edges of his eyes.

"I am surely not that," Morgana said, flatly.

Father Thomas marveled at the small patch, dropping to his knees to examine the herbs. While he was examining the delicate leaves on the lemon balm, Morgana dragged her hand through another small patch in the sand, revealing more soil. Within minutes, thin ferns sprouted up. When the ferns grew to her shoulder, Morgana twisted her hand through the stems and pulled up a fat, orange carrot. She handed it to Father Thomas.

He took it, running his hands over it. Morgana pulled her own carrot and sunk her teeth into it, trying to ease the hunger pains in her stomach.

"If you can do all this, why would Tiernan want to kill you?" Father Thomas asked. "Tales of Laird Forlan's brutality have reached the island, and I assumed his son was cut from the same cloth as he, but if you could work miracles like this, why would he kill you?"

"I don't think he was trying to kill me," Morgana said with the sad realization. "He was trying to scare me into marrying him."

"Marry him?" Father Thomas spat out in surprise. "That's quite a proposal. Ah, men and their lustful ways."

"Are you not a man?" Morgana asked.

"I am a holy man," Father Thomas returned with a smile. "And I cannot have you in the Priory, but I can find a place for you to stay in the village."

He had kind eyes and Morgana did not want to disappoint him, but she could not stay in the village. She could never go near anyone who would find out about her curse, or her gift, or whatever anyone wanted to call it. Mankind was a greedy beast who could never fill its bottomless pit. No one could know.

"I cannot. I cannot go to the village," Morgana pleaded, violently shaking her head. "I only wish to be alone, to be left in peace."

Father Thomas nodded.

"Very well," he said. "There is a small shed at the end of the easternmost wheat field. No one has used it in years. I am afraid it is humble, but you may stay there."

"Thank you," Morgana said.

She rushed to hug Father Thomas. She wrapped him in her arms. He hesitated a moment before embracing her tightly. It was his first contact with a woman and besides her late father, it was Morgana's first touch from a man who didn't want her exploited or dead. It was spellbinding for both of them.

For two years, Morgana stayed in the wheat shed on Holy Island. She grew vegetables and herbs for the Priory and the village. The gravediggers had not buried anyone in months. She was able to send cobblestones flying with a wave of her delicate hand. The roads were soon functioning, connecting the Priory and the village to the outer banks for fish carts.

Father Thomas continued to visit her and they talked about all things great and small. They talked about Iona, and Father Thomas's mother he had never known. They discussed the new ink Thomas was making and new ways to use the herbs Morgana had grown.

Their ideas and conversations carried their friendship along and Morgana cared for Father Thomas and all of the goodness he embodied. His works with medicine and his scholarly pursuits made Morgana long to see inside the Priory, to glimpse the wonders inside the stone building.

One day, she finally convinced Father Thomas to take her inside.

"I have no idea what the archbishop will say if he finds you inside here," he admitted, nervously rubbing his palms on his robe.

"Thomas, tell him I am an angel. You said I was," Morgana argued.

"I doubt the angels are this contrary," Father Thomas retorted, stroking his short beard.

Once they were inside the Priory, Morgana was rendered silent anyhow. The stone archways, the stained glass windows, the ornate architecture, they all took her breath away. There were so many shiny, metal objects.

"What metal is that?" Morgana asked, pointing to a cross adorned with rubies.

"It is gold," Father Thomas answered. "It is very valuable."

"I have never seen that before. Is this what heaven is like?" Morgana asked.

"I should hope not, it is rather drafty in here in the winter."

"I live in the wheat shed," Morgana returned.

"Yes, well," Father Thomas smiled.

The sky had been gray all day. A rolling thunderclap sent Thomas jumping halfway up the stone walls.

"We should go, but thank you," Morgana said.

She would never forget her trip inside the Priory. Father Thomas nodded and ushered her back into the wheat fields where she would go unnoticed. He had been venturing into the village and bringing gifts. A new shawl, a goat to keep, a small kettle to cook in. That night as she stirred her evening stew over the fire in her tiny hidden shack, gratitude filled her soul and she was sure she would never be happier than this, alone with her magic and one true friend.

Over the next few weeks, Father Thomas visited less often. He was anxious, claiming that he had seen a bad omen. He had heard whispers of the barbarian conquerors from the sea. The men were as tall as giants and as brutal as the devil himself. They raided and pillaged villages, leaving very few alive.

Father Thomas prayed day and night. He claimed to see dragons in the sky and beasts prowling the fields. They kept him from sleep. The monks told tales of the Gray King, Harek of Inksgate. They said he had killed so many that when he cleaned his axe, the waters ran red with blood for a week. They said he was as brutal a warrior as ever walked the earth. He was seven feet tall. He was impossible to kill. He was immortal. He could crush a man's head in one of his massive hands.

The next day, out of the clouds, a dragon's head appeared. Moments later, the head sailed through the fog, the helm of a ship with gray sails. Morgana gasped and started toward the Priory, but she was too late. Father Thomas rushed to her as smoke poured from the Priory windows.

She ran toward him across the wheat fields and as she did, she saw what followed. The Viking hoard was coming after him and the Gray King was leading them straight to Morgana.

CHAPTER 10

A New Girl in Town in an Attic Bedroom

Ivy shook her head in disbelief. She didn't think the athletic guy sitting next to her was going to say that.

"Tell me something you don't tell anyone," Ivy asked, sitting on the sandy shore with Onyx.

"I love playing chess," he confessed. "I'm really good at it too, I just-"

He shrugged, letting his sentence trail off. Ivy had seen guys like him, rugged outdoor loving dude-bro kind of guys. She swore she would never let herself get involved with one of them after seeing Everly fall for them time and time again, only to have her burning their gifts in bonfires six weeks later.

"You're kidding," Ivy said, eyeing him with a cynicism most girls her age wouldn't develop until college.

"No, I swear. Walk with me."

Onyx pulled her up by both hands. Ivy hopped up into his arms. She wasn't expecting him to be that strong.

"We're gonna go to the caves for a little bit!" Onyx called to Harbor and Olivia.

He grabbed a flashlight from his backpack lying on the beach.

"Oh, yeah?" Harbor asked with a raised eyebrow.

He and Olivia shared a look.

"What? Do you want me to livestream it? She'll be fine."

"Okay," Olivia drew out the word with a suspicious flick at the end.

"I didn't have to tell you where I was going," Ivy replied, putting her hands on her hips.

"You didn't tell me. Onyx did," Olivia raised her eyebrows.

Ivy just rolled her eyes. Onyx saluted to Olivia and led Ivy along back up the beach and through the trees, up to the road. Across the two lane road, an entrance to a hiking trail appeared. A small wooden sign warned, "Don't go into the woods alone." Onyx grabbed Ivy's hand.

"Wait," Ivy hesitated.

In the middle of the road, a small turtle dug at the asphalt, trying to cross the road to get to the lake. Ivy checked for cars and then scooped up the turtle and returned him to the grassy safety on the other side of the road. When the lone pickup truck driving on the deserted road had passed, Ivy skipped across the street.

"There," she declared with a triumphant smile.

"Ivy Jasper, turtle rescuer," Onyx smiled.

"You have to! I always do. They're too slow."

Onyx wrapped his arm around her. They walked a ways into the woods until they came to a small opening in the side of the rocky sloping hill. The mouth of the cave seemed to pour cool air into the woods.

It was a little dark, so Onyx popped the flashlight open to change it into a lantern, illuminating the darkness of the cave. Light spilled into every crevice of the stone. He opened his backpack to grab what looked like a rubber mat and a bag of small people, but in pixelated form, like an old school video game. When he unrolled the mat, Ivy could see that it was a board and the rubber figures were chess pieces.

"I designed it and printed it on my mom's 3-D printer at work," Onyx said. "She prints jewelry holders and stuff, but she let me print my chess set."

"Wow," Ivy said. "So, in addition to baseball, you play chess?"

"And football," Onyx answered. "I've come up with some really cool plays with my chess set. We won a big game with one of my plays last year. I've been working on some new ones for this season."

"That's awesome," Ivy glowed.

She sat down next to Onyx and the chess set, feeling his long arm drape around her.

"I know how to play," she offered.

Chess was a regular thing in the *Jardin du Tuileries* where she spent so many days waiting for her mom's treatments to end. She had picked up the game and a good amount of French by playing with the retired citizens of Paris.

"I know this is the king, and this is the queen, but I don't know the other names in English," she frowned.

"Wow, really? You'd play with me? Okay," Onyx beamed, and rushed to set up the board, as though Ivy might change her mind. "You don't think it's lame?"

"It's been around since the seventh century. How is that lame?" Ivy asked.

Onyx's eyes flashed and a huge smile lit up his face.

"Okay, this is the *tour*," Ivy pointed to the rook.

"That's the rook," Onyx said.

"Rook," she repeated. "And this is the *fou*, and the *cavalier*. And I know the pawn."

"Bishop, and knight," Onyx finished. "That's so cool that you learned to play chess in French."

"I didn't have much to do while I was waiting on my mom to get better."

Onyx nodded.

"Do you want to talk about it?" he asked.

Ivy shook her head.

"Let's just play."

The game lasted longer than most of Onyx's chess matches. Ivy was pretty good, but Onyx spent a lot of his downtime playing on his chess app and going through scenarios while working out. He pictured the other football players as knights, rooks, and pawns. He couldn't wait to get back to camp to test out his strategies.

"Okay, you win," Ivy giggled.

"We should get back, it's late," Onyx said with a twinge of a frown. "But you'll be close by at your new house, and we can see each other all the time. You okay with that?"

Ivy nodded. Onyx held out a hand to help her up. Once she was standing, she leaned in to wrap her arms around him. He smelled amazing.

"Good," Onyx said, leaning on one of the rocks in the cave and pulling Ivy close to him. "Because I really like you. I mean it. I really, really like you."

"Me?" Ivy asked.

"Yes, you."

Onyx kissed her forehead. Ivy leaned into his chest. It had been a long time since someone really liked her, and maybe even worse, it had been a long time since she cared.

The next day Ivy smiled, blinking into the sunshine, with the window rolled down in the backseat of her parents' car. She remembered the moment with Onyx, looking down and smiling at the text he had just sent.

-I'm on my way home! I can't stop thinking about you!

Ivy bit her lip, trying to stifle a huge grin. She left with her parents the day before Onyx to move into their new house in Heavener. Her parents were going to begin researching the runestone in Runestone Park. They were looking for anything significant to stop Phillips Petroleum from building an oil pipeline straight through the park, but because of the contract, something major had to be found, something like a historic site of artifacts or a new species, but all anyone had found were the stones and those could be moved. So, Max and Camille Jasper had been hired by the preservation society to find something to stop the pipeline.

It didn't take long to move into their beautifully renovated, but tiny shotgun house. The small house sat on a patch of land set back from the road next to a stream. Like most shotgun houses, the living room and kitchen took up the front part of the house, with a bathroom in the middle, and a bedroom in the back of the house. A laundry room had been added and the attic had been converted to another loft bedroom.

Ivy set out all her clothes, books, and craft supplies. She made most of her own jewelry and hardly ever wore any clothes she bought without making alterations of some sort. Clothes are built for tall people, she concluded, so I guess I'll just have to make adjustments.

The next day, she and her parents were driving around exploring the town. After lunch at Bud's Bread Shed, they drove by a shop her mom insisted on popping into.

It was a little white stucco shop painted with teal and fuchsia accents. A vintage sign adorned the top and different antique doors surrounded much of the outside.

Sweet Tea and Tiffany, that sounds familiar, Ivy thought to herself. While Camille wandered in the shop, Ivy looked around the register area. Photos of Onyx at all ages surrounded the register. There were photos of a little girl with freckles, too. That must be Bailey, Ivy assumed.

I knew it, Ivy squealed inside. This is Onyx's mom's store.

"Hey, y'all! Sorry, I've been in the back with some markdowns."

A beautiful woman with long, glossy hair came bursting through swinging doors from the back of the shop. She had the same dark charcoal eyes as Onyx, but wasn't much taller than Ivy. One glance at the giant man in one of the pictures revealed the secret to Onyx's height.

"What a lovely store," Camille gushed.

"Thank you," the woman radiated a big smile. "I'm Tiffany, Tiffany Rainwater, this my little store, and that's my little girl, Bailey, and my not so little boy, Onyx."

"I met him at the lake," Ivy said, her excitement brimming over. "He was with my cousin and her boyfriend."

"Harbor and Olivia?" Tiffany asked. "Small world! We just had them out to the house a few months ago. She's so sweet and Harbor is a hoot. I'll have to tell Onyx you stopped by."

"He just texted me," Ivy smiled.

"Lucky him," Tiffany quipped.

"Ivy, what about this for freshman orientation this afternoon?" Camille called from the clothing section.

She held up a cute romper, white with maroon and dusty rose florals. Ivy grinned and nodded.

"That would look adorable on you!" Tiffany gushed. "You said you had freshman orientation today?"

"Yes," Ivy replied. "I thought that Heavener had its own high school, but it's just kindergarten through eighth grade. I'll be going to Big Cabin with Onyx."

"That's right, the Heavener kids do go to Big Cabin for high school. Oklahoma schools are funny," Tiffany shrugged, then added in a low voice, "and totally underfunded."

She had to get this girl out of the store so she could call Onyx. What on Earth did he do to get a girl like her to go all goo goo eyed over him anyway, Tiffany wondered. For the past year, Onyx had just been going through the motions. Tiffany felt for him, but didn't know what to do. Now that she thought about it though, he did seem to have more life in his voice when he called the other day.

Ivy and her mom paid for the outfit and left. Tiffany almost tripped over herself, running to the back to dig her phone out of her purse. It rang three times, but she knew her son would pick up. He always picked up for his mama.

"Hey Mom!"

Yep, Onyx was happy and it must have something to do with the pretty blonde in Tiffany's newest floral romper. Hey, at least the girl had style.

"Don't you 'hey mom' me, Onyx Jason Rainwater. What gorgeous blonde freshman did I just meet who says she knows you?"

"That's Ivy, my girlfriend. Well, my almost girlfriend. Isn't she awesome?" Onyx asked.

"Um, yes, but there is the fact that you already have a scary crazy stalker girlfriend who is going to murder my only son when she finds out about Miss Down-to-Her-Waist-Blonde-Hair."

"She likes chess and speaks French, too. She's amazing and I have been meaning to end things with Madison for a long time. It's just so hard because she's so nuts. Look, I'm just going to to break up with Madison today when I get home and then everything will be great."

"Mmm hmm," Tiffany smirked. "But here's the thing. Ivy has freshman orientation today."

"Yeah, at Heavener. She told me." Onyx replied, unaware.

"No, at Big Cabin. Did you forget that Heavener only goes through eighth grade and feeds into Big Cabin for high school?"

"Wait, what?"

Onyx panicked as he let that sink in.

"And the sophomore class president is running freshman orientation."

Oh. Crap. Madison. Onyx may have dropped the phone.

If Ivy meets Madison, I'm dead. Everyone in a six mile radius is dead.

CHAPTER 11

How Could You?

Madison Vine tugged a manicured hand down her stick-straight brown hair, feeling for any waves or imperfections. She adjusted her diamond stud earrings and smoothed on some plain lip gloss.

She smiled. Her boyfriend since middle school, Onyx, had planned to make her some stupid scrapbook for Valentine's Day, but she told him not to even think about it. She had ordered the perfect, understated earrings online and had them shipped to his house. How else was she going to get the Valentine's Day present she wanted?

Madison turned and plastered on a serene smile, looking down her nose at all the freshmen coming in for orientation. That is, until she saw the one freshman worth her attention. She smiled to Trystan Crimi, the freshman football team's quarterback. He was a year younger than her and didn't have as successful a career as Onyx, but he was organized, accomplished, and really nice to look at. His dirty blonde hair curled around his ears at the perfect length and his clothes were polished, country club perfect. He gave her a polite nod, then made his way into the auditorium.

The rest of the freshmen just looked dumb and confused, shuffling in like cattle. They were so lucky to have Madison organizing the orientation. After all, she had set up tables for the foreign language nerds, the band geeks, and the worst of the worst, the chess club. Hopefully some of these losers would join the band so someone would play "Louie, Louie" at the football games. What else did the cheer squad have to stunt to? The new speaker system wasn't in place yet and she wasn't using some crappy boom box. Madison sighed and examined her manicure until she heard heels clicking across the tile.

Well, what fresh slut face is this? Madison whipped around, staring daggers at a girl in a white floral romper and wedges. Half of her hair was done up in a knot on top of her head and the other half fell in loose waves down to her waist. A rose gold boyfriend watch swung loosely on her wrist and she twisted a long vintage bronze necklace in her fingers.

Madison stifled the flash of jealousy and pasted the smile back on. She watched the girl all through the orientation presentation. She watched Trystan catch his breath and stop mid-speech when he noticed her sitting in the third row. Madison's eyes followed her as she mingled with some newspaper geeks, band nerds, and even stopped by the chess club table out in the hall. Who was this girl?

Moments later, Madison broke her concentration when Onyx came sprinting through the hall, heading toward none other than romper skank. What was he doing?

Madison stepped in front of Onyx, startling him.

"What are you doing here? Trystan already talked about freshman football."

"Trystan? The kid that always wears the boat shoes?"

"He's the quarterback."

Madison placed herself firmly between Onyx and the crowd of incoming freshmen. The last thing she needed was her boyfriend screwing everything up. Onyx was the best looking sophomore at Big Cabin, a football star, and he made good grades, so Madison figured she was set with him, but he had the worst habit of showing up when he wasn't supposed to and trying to have his own stupid ideas. Then there was the time he said he wanted to play chess. Madison just about blew a gasket.

"We need to talk," Onyx said, obviously out of breath.

"No, we most certainly do not need to talk. You need to go home," Madison instructed.

"No, Madison, I'm not-"

"Onyx!"

The blonde girl was sauntering up to Madison's boyfriend and she was not going to have any of it. Madison stepped in front of her.

"Hi!" Madison beamed a friendly smile. "Welcome to Big Cabin! We're so happy you're here. I'm Madison Vine, sophomore class president. Are you a freshman this year?"

"Um, yes. I'm Ivy. I know-"

"Oh, you know my boyfriend, Onyx?"

Ivy stopped. Her chest pounded and seemed to cave in on what used to be her heart. The words she almost said were stuck in her throat. Spots danced at the edges of her vision. She turned to look at Onyx. A look of pure horror crossed his face.

She knew it. There was no way she had met the guy of her dreams. At that moment, she knew everyone was right. Laur was right when he said she was just someone to pass the time. Everly was right when she said there was no way Ivy could ever be the pretty girl. She would always be just the frumpy, ugly sidekick. What was she doing in this stupid outfit anyway?

The least she could do was just save things for Onyx. At least she felt good about herself for a little while.

"Ivy, wait," Onyx pleaded.

"No, it's fine," Ivy looked down, but then looked up, smiling a tight smile. "My bike chain broke, on the way here, but Onyx helped me fix it. That's all."

"Well, he's a great guy!" Madison beamed.

Ivy nodded, then, realizing the gravity of the situation, stuck out her hand to Onyx. Her voice cooled.

"It was nice to meet you. Just now."

We're not meant for handshakes, Onyx had told her, by the lake, the first night he kissed her.

"Ivy, it's not what you think," Onyx pleaded, refusing to shake her outstretched hand, the one he had held watching fireworks.

"Yeah, it could be the bike chain, or one of the gears, or the pedal. I don't know," Ivy said, her voice breaking.

She took her hand back, turned on a heel, and walked away.

"Well, that clears things up," Madison said, brushing imaginary crumbs off her monogrammed gingham shorts.

"It's over, Madison," Onyx said. "I'm sorry, but we're not starting this year dating or anything, like no. You and I are done. I don't even know what I was thinking."

"How could you?" Madison hissed, yanking Onyx into a hallway. "Who do you think you are? I practically made you. You would be nothing without me."

Madison was seething. Her smile and bubbly attitude had evaporated.

"Oh yeah, Madison. Like you make all those touchdowns and win games for Big Cabin? Nope, that's me. It takes everyone about five seconds to see through you. I should have broken up with you sooner, but I didn't want to deal with your crazy, but now it's worth dealing with."

Madison was silent. She turned and strutted back to orientation, but Onyx knew he would be dealing with it later. For now, he had to find Ivy.

Onyx ran out to his truck and circled the school. He was three months away from getting his license, but he took his black Silverado out anyway. Ivy was worth breaking the rules. Or laws, whatever.

Onyx found her riding her bike, barefoot, with her shoes in her bike basket. She was crying. Onyx choked back his own tears. He had wanted to break up with Madison in person, but he wanted to be with Ivy at the lake. He wanted to be with her now. She should be in his passenger's seat instead of in tears on her bike, but she wasn't and it was his fault.

"Ivy, can you please stop? Please?" Onyx called out the window, driving slowly beside her.

"No! Leave me alone!" Ivy screamed back.

Her makeup was streaked in dark trails down her cheeks. Her face was pink and blotchy.

"Please just get in and let me take you home."

"Leave me alone!" Ivy cried and pedaled faster.

"Ivy, please!"

Onyx called after her, but she turned off, into the woods where he couldn't follow her with his truck. Onyx slammed on the brakes and slumped over the steering wheel. He couldn't follow Ivy into the woods and he couldn't make her see how sorry he was, but he could stay away from Madison, and not give her any more power over his life or his decisions, ever. Maybe, in time, Ivy would find a way to trust him again.

The dried reeds snapped at the tops of Ivy's feet as she pedaled into a grassy meadow at the edge of the woods. She didn't know this area. She checked her phone. No service. Ivy sobbed and tried to catch her breath. She already had a text from Onyx from when she left school.
-I was going to break up with her when I got back. I'm sorry. Please talk to me.
Ivy cried over her bike basket. Her breaths came out in racked sobs. Through her tears, she could make out a dark shape at the edge of the woods. Ivy swiped her tears away.
A woman in a black hooded robe stood at the edge of the forest, looking directly at Ivy. Her face was lined with dark markings and her red hair spilled out from her hood. Despite the heat, she wore a fox pelt around her shoulders.
Ivy stood, paralyzed, unable to move, but shaking from crying and now from fear. The woman was beautiful and terrifying.
"The Stone Witch," Ivy whispered. "She's real."
The ground under Ivy's feet began to

tremble. Ivy gripped her bike, looking around the meadow, with no idea what to do, but as suddenly as it started, the tremors stopped. Ivy looked back to the woods.

"Who are you?"

Ivy knelt down and placed her palm to the ground, the way her mother showed her. She asked the question not into the air with her voice, but into the earth itself and the earth seemed to echo its answer back to her.

Morgana.

CHAPTER 12

From Holy Island To Hell on Earth, 1131 A.D.

Father Thomas was shouting at her but she couldn't run. Morgana was rooted to the earth, watching the Viking hoard chase after Thomas. The Gray King was astoundingly tall as Thomas had said, yet two giant-like warriors, taller than the king, flanked him on either side. Twelve or so more followed behind, clad in battle worn leather, carrying heavy shields, iron swords, and battle axes.

Morgana thought they would be making more noise. Thomas said they sounded like demons when they tore through towns, raiding and pillaging. The Priory was on fire, flames licking at the sky, smoke pouring from the windows.

Yet, the Gray King was silent and so was his raiding party. His coal black eyes fixed on her. Unlike the other long haired warriors, his hair was cut short, the dark brown flecked mostly gray.

His skin was tanned and weather beaten from the salt water spray of the ocean and even though his hair was half gray, his beard was black, streaked with the smallest bit of charcoal. Only his shield was painted gray. The rest of the warriors carried shields in a sickening blood red.

"Morgana run!"

But she would not run. Thomas once told her that the Vikings had a saying. "Run from battle and you will only die tired." Morgana was tired. She was half dead inside and she would not allow the heathens to take Lindsfarne and she certainly wouldn't allow them to kill Thomas.

Morgana focused all her energy, snaking her arms out, her limbs growing like tree trunks. She sailed her new limbs around Thomas, heading straight toward the Viking warriors. She grabbed the nearest warrior with a nightmarish hand of branches. The man was at least six feet tall, and with gritted teeth and iron will, she used her newly grown vine of an arm to fling him over the cliffs and out to sea.

"Shield wall!" the Gray King shouted to his warriors.

A wall of shields went up, red with one gray circle. Morgana retracted her arms. She raised a palm and every single bit of the wood in the shields turned to dust.

"I will kill you," Morgana shouted. "Leave us in peace!"

"I cannot do that, Stone Witch," the Gray King shouted.

He tossed the shell of what was his shield aside and continued to stalk toward Father Thomas. Morgana's thoughts turned to rage. I will rip your heart out of your chest if you touch him, she seethed. The Gray King grabbed Father Thomas by the collar of his robe and slung him to the ground. Morgana stretched her arms out again, growing them toward the king.

"Cast the net!"

As soon as he gave the orders, four warriors to the back of the party threw a metal net from weights attached to the four corners. Morgana watched in horror as it silhouetted against the sky. Once the iron touched her skin, her limbs retracted as her powers seemed to evaporate into the air itself.

"I am King Harek of Inksgate," the man said with little passion in his voice.

The Gray King loomed over her. He held onto Father Thomas. One of the warriors held a sword to his throat. Harek peeled back the iron net, allowing Morgana a few moments to catch her breath.

"How did you find me?" Morgana asked, straining against the iron.

"I raided Castle Dirleton," Harek answered," and found only the cook and the servants. One sailor made it back to tell them about the Stone Witch, her capture, her torture, and her sentence.

He told that in place of a witch's trial, she destroyed an entire warship and killed Forlan MacNagaulla and all of his warriors."

"I will not destroy anything on your behalf," Morgana hissed and struggled uselessly against the net.

"I do not ask you to destroy anything, Stone Witch. The cook and the servants heard tales that you could make things grow. Thus I ask you, come with us to Inksgate. Make things grow," Harek paused, unsheathing a massive longsword. He kicked Father Thomas to the ground and placed the sword at the nape if his neck. "Or watch him die."

"Morgana, no. Do not go with the heathens. They are barbarians, no better than animals. I am prepared to die. My soul will be saved."

The Gray King's giant, veined hand gripped the sword, claw-like. His arms were like muscled tree trunks. He would surely take Father Thomas's head cleanly off his shoulders. His strong jaw was set, betraying no emotions.

"Yes," Morgana answered simply, ignoring Thomas. "Yes, you have your answer."

The Gray King peeled back part of the net and locked iron chains around her wrists.

"No, please!"

Father Thomas begged them not to take her. She saw at once in his eyes how deeply he cared for her. Harek left Thomas in the middle of the wheat field but he left him alive. As it turns out, the Gray King did not want to take Lindsfarne or any of its precious metals or jewels. He only came for one thing. He only wanted the Stone Witch.

Thomas's pleading face was the last thing she saw before one of the warriors snapped a black hood over her head, threw her over his mountainous shoulder, and dragged her to the boat.

Morgana spent three weeks locked in a cell on the largest longship in the king's fleet. He slept outside of her cell every night. He didn't sleep much. He looked at the sky often. Every day, he would chain her hands with iron and let her walk about the boat. One day when she had grown tired of her cell, she snapped at him. They were the first words she had spoken to him since she told him she would go with him.

"You do not have to do that. You do not have to lock me in there. I am not going to escape. We are in the middle of an ocean. You are as dim witted as you look."

The Gray King didn't speak. He stared at her with penetrating black eyes. A scar ran from his cheek through the left side of his lips. Morgana found her eyes lingering over his lips, but stopped the treasonous thought as soon as it started. The king seemed to be taking in every bit of her marked face.

"Can you speak, imbecile? Do I frighten you so? Does my face scare you?"

"I am King Harek, the Gray King of

Inksgate. Son of Rollnar, Ruler of the Riverlands, but you may address me as Harek."

Morgana and Harek stared at each other for a few seconds with nothing but the sound of the waves between them. He broke the silence and leaned close to her.

"You do not scare me. Your face does not scare me. I have seen more in battle than you can imagine in your wildest nightmares. I am not frightened of a tiny girl with red hair and I do not lock you in. I lock them out."

Harek motioned to his warriors on the deck of his longship. They looked at her like the dragon at the front of the ship looked out to the sea. Hungry and uncaring what humanity lied before them.

"Well then," Morgana smoothed her hands over her ragged dress as though it were a fine silk. "I am Morgana. You may address me as Morgana. My mother was murdered by a terrible, pompous man and my father was worked to death by a selfish, greedy laird and I am already dead. I hate you. I will always hate you and one day I will kill you. I promise you. Do you think you have to protect me from them?"

Morgana motioned to the warriors. They were dirty and weather beaten from their days on the ship, but they still looked at her as though they wanted to tear her limb from limb.

"Take off my irons," Morgana command to Harek.

He didn't look like someone who was used to taking commands but he removed the chains and laid them down in the bottom of the ship.

"Now let me show you why you don't have to protect me," Morgana said. She turned to the warriors. They had been battle tested by Harek himself and by some of the fiercest armies in the known world. "Who would lay a finger on the Stone Witch against her will?"

The tallest Viking warrior sneered and took a step forward. He was a giant with pale blonde hair, dreadlocked down his back, and a muscular body that blocked out the sun when he stood up in front of Morgana.

As he grabbed his sword and twirled it in his hand, laughing, Morgana pulsed her arms out as sharp trunks, piercing the warrior once through the heart and once through the stomach. He looked almost surprised as Morgana's arms grew through his torso, wrapped around him, and pierced both of his sides. Morgana looked directly at Harek as she steadied herself on the deck of the longship and tore his finest warrior apart straight down the middle. Blood and organs splattered on the deck.

She deposited both halves of his fresh corpse into the ocean. The sharks began to circle. When her arms returned to normal, they were slick with blood. The warriors all drew their swords and waited for the order from Harek. Surely she couldn't kill all of them at once.

The Gray King was silent.

"He is in Valhalla," Harek finally remarked and waved the rest of the men about their business.

The men grumbled and angrily spat on the deck of the ship, but obeyed the order. Harek gazed out to the sea and then settled on Morgana. He paused, gathering himself.

"Do not do that again, Stone Witch," he said in a low voice, and then added, "Morgana. Do not do that again."

Harek then grabbed the iron chains that had once bound her and dropped them into the ocean. They sunk down to the sea floor, where they rest to this very day.

Three weeks later, Morgana woke up, blinking into the sun. The boat was still. When she sat up, she noticed there was a dock next to her and swords pointing directly at her.

"You must come with us," a smaller warrior said. "Forgive me. I am Arin of Inksgate, brother to Harek. He has charged me with bringing you ashore, my lady."

Morgana did not fight him. She walked ashore to Inksgate with eight men surrounding her, pointing the tip of their swords at her, escorting her down the wide dock. She pulled the hood of her cloak over her head, lest anyone see her face. At the end of the wooden dock, Harek waited for her with tired eyes and sunken, hollow cheeks.

Morgana peered around him and gasped at what she saw.

There were few women and children, even fewer older citizens. They were thin and gaunt. Their skin was gray and there was no life behind their eyes. The land was dead with famine. The waters of the Riverlands ran foul. A large mass grave, full with bodies sat open. The villagers didn't have strength enough to bury their dead. A haggard old woman sat counting out single grains for the remaining villagers. They had come within a few grains of starvation.

"My God, Harek," Morgana fell to her knees, tears spilling out of her eyes at the wretched scene.

"Will you help us?" he asked.

He strode toward her and sunk down on one knee. Morgana was in tears, gasping for breath, wracked with guilt and horror at what she saw. Harek took her marked face in one of his large hands.

"Morgana, please? Will you help us? We have nothing else to hope for."

She nodded through hazy tears. Morgana stepped off the dock and placed one hand on the ground. The infection in the earth was so horrid, she shuddered, holding back from retching. She inhaled and sucked the rot from the ground. When she had pulled the bile from the land, she exhaled out the cursed famine, up into the air, letting the winds carry it away.

When she was done, she placed a palm to the earth, sending a line of pure light to a tree not far off the shore. The tree vibrated with being and burst open with fruit. Harek, his army, and all the villagers looked at each other in astonishment and then, the people of Inksgate ran to grasp fruit from the tree. The adults grabbed fruit for their hungry children. They sliced off pieces to carry to the sick and the old.

Morgana fell over, exhausted from the effort. She didn't feel Harek pick her up and carry her off the shore. She didn't hear him sobbing with delirium and relief.

CHAPTER 13

THE PIPELINE

Jay Rainwater pointed to a wrench just out of his reach. Onyx grabbed the wrench and handed it to his dad. He was working on one of their vintage motorcycles. They each had one. Onyx rode the bike ever since he got his motorcycle license at fourteen years old. He had been riding the hills and back roads of Heavener and Big Cabin for a month, but he hadn't seen the person he wanted to see the most, riding around on her yellow bicycle.

Ivy eluded him at school. She spent most of her time in the freshman building and the newspaper room. Onyx scoured *The Doghouse*, the school's newspaper, for anything she had written, but so far there was nothing, only a few photo credits. Every football game, he looked up to the stands for her. She stood dutifully taking pictures for the paper, but she was gone before the team left the field.

"You've been having a great season, son," Jay said, bringing Onyx back to reality.

His dad was right. He had been having a great season. Onyx was his varsity team's star tight end. With his new height and muscular build, he hadn't lost any speed or agility. After four games, he was sitting at five hundred and sixty yards with forty two receptions and seven touchdowns. He plowed through every defense he came across. Big Cabin was undefeated.

Still, looking out to the stands and not seeing Ivy had him feeling pretty defeated. Flip and D'Mario both had a slew of girls waiting to talk to them after the games. His friend Remy Oliver, the team's cornerback and rodeo clown in training, had a whole cheering section. Madison made a big deal about ignoring him and spouting off about how her new boyfriend from Broken Bow would have run circles around Onyx. He didn't care, she was easy to ignore. She had ignored him most of the time they were going out. I just showed up for pictures, Onyx thought with an ironic smile.

Everything was humming along for him, except for one critical part of his day. Every day, he would wait at the bottom of the freshman steps for Ivy to finish up her English class and make her way down to lunch. She hadn't had any trouble making friends on the newspaper. She would give him a quick look and then just turn back to her friends to talk. A few days ago, she gave him a small smile. It was all the motivation he needed not to give up.

Maybe it was just like chess. Forethought wins the game.

On the other hand, there was drama from Madison. For the first week of school, she had refused to acknowledge the break up. She sent herself flowers from Onyx, bought herself new jewelry, but most everyone had caught on. Miraculously, she had a new boyfriend who went to another school within the week. Onyx was relieved, but he had a feeling he wasn't out of the woods yet. Madison might change her tune if Ivy ever started talking to him again.

"Are you okay Dad?"

Onyx was picking up a worried vibe from his dad. He had been nervous all week.

"Phillips Oil is starting construction on the pipeline next week. They're going through the forest and only an endangered species or a burial ground can stop it at this point," Jay answered.

He was nervous. None of them knew what that meant for the park. They were routing the pipeline around the side of the park, away from the thermal pools, but there were hundreds of species of animals who called the forest their home. Only the discovery of a new species or a burial ground could reroute the pipeline, and so far, there were only species registered as prolific and no bodies buried in the area, only the stone statues of the warriors carved so long ago.

"They're moving one of the smaller runestones tomorrow, as well. The Jaspers are helping with it. They're moving it to the preservation society. If we could only find the salt crane, we could preserve the area, but everyone thinks it's extinct. I know it isn't. I know it's out there."

"Guys!" Bailey shouted into the garage. "Mom said to come in for dinner. I'm gonna eat all your food, Onyx!"

Onyx just laughed. There was no way that Bailey, his mom, or his dad combined could eat all his food.

"And I'm gonna tell that blonde girl that you stalk on Facebook how much you totally love her!"

"Bay, get your butt outta here," Onyx teased.

Ivy knew how Onyx felt. He sent her a text once a day, everyday.

Bailey stuck only her tiny rear end back into the house and gave it a shake.

"My butt is out! My butt is out!"

Onyx laughed and threw an empty water bottle at her. She stuck her tongue out at him and ran back into the kitchen.

"You kids," Jay laughed, shaking his head. "Hey, Bailey Jade, shut the door!"

Everyone was quiet at dinner, allowing Jay the headspace to process what would happen in the morning. The next few weeks held nervous energy for the Rainwaters. That night, Onyx fell into a troubled sleep. Who could say what damage the pipeline would do? And what would it take for Ivy to talk to him again? The questions seemed to swirl around him, dragons flying in the skies of his dreams. Onyx woke before the sunrise on the day that the pipeline construction began, nervous about the days to come.

CHAPTER 14

Publications and Reservations

Out of nowhere that morning, Flip came running up to Onyx and jumped halfway up his side. It was no small feat considering Onyx's size. Flip grabbed Onyx by the shirt and tugged violently. He didn't make much of an impact, but he was trying.

"Onyx, man, you need to read this! Look at this! Do you see this, man?"

Flip waved the newspaper in Onyx's face. He stopped periodically to hop up and down and then wave the paper again. The whole hallway turned to look at them. It was one very impressive flip out from Flip Dominguez.

"He can't see it if you keep waving it around like that," their friend Caleb pointed out.

Always the voice of reason and Big Cabin's resident math genius, Caleb Roy was soft spoken, but hardly ever wrong.

"Caleb, man, stop hassling me. I'm trying to show him," Flip retorted, crumpling up the very newspaper in question and throwing it at Caleb.

"Here," Caleb smiled a wide, knowing smile and handed Onyx a fresh copy of the latest issue of *The Doghouse*.

The headline read, "Rainwater Running the Show" with five amazing action shots of Onyx barreling through the opposing team's defense into the end zone. The article was well written and highlighted all of his big moments from their first four games.

"Do you know what this means?" Flip shouted down the hall to half the sophomore class at Big Cabin.

"Shut up, Flip I swear," Onyx cut his empty threat short, feeling a hand on shoulder.

He turned around to see Ivy, all blonde wavy hair and shy looks in a mint green t-shirt dress with slip on sneakers.

"I didn't know if you'd like it," she said, shrugging her shoulders and staring at her shoes.

Onyx looked back at D'Mario, Caleb, and Flip.

"Well, I can see when I ain't needed. Come on fellas," D'Mario said, turning around.

"Bye D'Mario," Flip waved.

"You too, Flip. Come on," Caleb motioned, running a hand through his white blonde hair.

"Awe, you always boss me," Flip grumbled on his way down the hall.

Onyx watched the crew make their way to Remy standing down the hall and turned back to Ivy, hoping she wasn't a mirage. She was still there, clutching her own copy of the paper. Ivy rocked back and forth on her heels smiling a tight lipped smile.

"Can I-"

Onyx trailed off the question. He brought his arms out, his wide wingspan waiting to swoop down on Ivy the moment she gave the okay. Onyx grinned when she nodded and scooped her up into a big, long, and much overdue hug. Her shoes lifted at least a foot off the floor. He didn't notice the entire hallway stop to stare at them.

"I missed you, Ive," Onyx whispered into her hair.

"I know, I missed you, too," Ivy said, her voice wavering and then breaking into shaking sobs. "I'm sorry. I'm so sorry. I know you were just trying to do the right thing. I shouldn't have been so stubborn. I was so dumb. I mean, from what everyone told me, Madison pretty much ignored you, too. I can't believe I was acting just like her, I can't- I would never- I don't know. I'm so sorry."

Onyx held her and let her say what she needed to say, letting go of a month's worth of unsaid feelings. She cried into his t-shirt, a big wet spot growing on the heather gray fabric.

"You're always in gray and black," Ivy said.

She kept her arms wrapped up around his neck.

"Not everyone can have style like you," Onyx said.

He squatted down until they were faced to face. Ivy laughed as he picked her up and held her over his head, not losing sight of her face. She kicked her sneakered feet and squealed peals of laughter that echoed through the commons. Onyx finally put her down and shook out his left arm, spinning the large watch on his wrist. He draped his arm around Ivy.

"Okay shortness, are you gonna let me walk you to class now?" he asked.

"What? You don't even know my schedule," Ivy stared incredulously through thick eyelashes.

"Oh, yes I do," Onyx laughed. "You have History and then Bio and then Newspaper."

"You had Caleb look it up!" Ivy accused.

Caleb had tech first hour and had been instrumental in revamping the school's software. He coded it himself using bit of open source code and some he had written himself. Everyone knew that he could log in and see whatever he wanted.

"Not tellin'," Onyx held up his palms. "Can I see you this weekend?"

Onyx stopped and asked the question. Everyone would be going to a bonfire at The Swamp after the football game, a marshy area on Remy's family's land that was technically in another county. Nefarious activity aside, Onyx was dying to take Ivy to hang out with his friends. He only recently began to hang out with them again after breaking up with Madison. There was no way she would ever go within five thousand feet of The Swamp. As she put it, she had a reputation to protect.

More than that, he wanted to take her hiking in the woods, the most peaceful place he knew. He gauged her reaction after he asked. She smiled and nodded, grabbing his hand.

"I can't wait."

Onyx smiled back. Neither could he.

"Onyx!"

Remy was standing on top of a pile of hay bales, wearing a cowboy hat and a glow necklace, and waving a plastic sword. Music blared from car speakers and a roaring bonfire illuminated the entire area, cleared in the trees.

"You ready for this, Ive?"

Ivy nodded. She was ready. She had been dabbling in more advanced magic. She could disintegrate wood and suck the oxygen out of a space for about twenty seconds, very effectively putting out a fire. You can never have too much fire safety with a cousin like Ashley Nirran, Ivy concluded. Everyone was more than safe around Ivy and fire.

Onyx parked the bike and unrolled a thick blanket. Ivy smiled, sat down, and snuggled into his side. Onyx had a great game. His left hand was a little mangled from smashing it in between a helmet and the forty yard line, but Ivy was able to run her hands over his hand and heal any of the torn skin.

"What is that, Ivy Jasper?" Onyx asked.

"Just something I can do," she smiled.

Onyx shifted on the ground. Her large bag had rolled from the hillside into his back.

"And what's in there, Ive?" he asked. "You're full of surprises."

Ivy smiled and produced a bottle of vodka from her bag. When no one was looking, she blinked it out of the liquor store. A quick close of her eyelids and it was safely in her bag. Vodka is mostly liquid potatoes, after all. Onyx laughed and shook his head.

"What? It's a bonfire. It's marshmallow flavored vodka."

"I didn't say anything," Onyx said through a smile. "You officially can't compare yourself to Madison, like ever again, okay?"

"Okay, but I did fix their broken window at the back of the store as payment. I'm not a thief."

Onyx laughed as he twisted the top off the vodka a took a big swig.

"Not bad," he shrugged and handed the bottle to Ivy.

She took a few drinks, then replaced the cap and set it beside her. Onyx leaned over and kissed her with the sting of vodka still in his throat. Ivy kissed him back, feeling his full lips against hers. She first noticed them smiling out from under his baseball cap at the tournament. If you had told her two months later she would be wrapped up in his arms at a bonfire after he had scored two touchdowns that night, she would have stamped you certifiably insane. Ivy leaned her head on Onyx's chest.

"Whoa, whoa now! What do we have here?" D'Mario sang, his own can of beer perched atop another unopened beer.

D'Mario, Caleb, Flip, and Remy balanced on the tree roots surrounding Onyx and Ivy's blanket. Ivy took one last swig of vodka and handed the bottle to Onyx, who drained about a quarter of the bottle. He capped it and tossed it to Remy.

"Marshmallow vodka for your marshmallow ass, Rem. Think you can actually make a tackle next game?"

Remy laughed and downed a long swig from the bottle. Onyx shook his head and led Ivy down to the marsh. He held her close to him as the fireflies buzzed around them.

"Kiss me again," Ivy smiled, looking up.

"No, you've been drinking." Onyx replied, kissing her forehead.

It took all of his resolve to stop himself from kissing her until midnight when they both had to be home, but he didn't want to if she was the slightest bit out of her element. Ivy laughed and pointed out the fireflies. Onyx drove them home after a few hours and a few bottles of water.

"Tomorrow, you promise?" he asked.

"I promise!" Ivy called behind her.

They were going hiking so Onyx could show her his world, the most quiet, peaceful place on Earth and maybe, if he was lucky, he would get a glimpse into her world as well.

"I don't know about this," Ivy said, the next morning.

"Having second thoughts, Ive?" Onyx asked.

"No. It's just early," Ivy whined.

The fall chill in the air set in and Ivy opted for a chunky sweater and high wasted jeans. Her hair was a mess and sleepy eyes peeked out from the sweater's large turtleneck. She held onto Onyx's waist on the four wheeler that drove them deeper into the forest.

Onyx had been up with the sun, jogging and doing some light boxing in the garage. Ivy had been sleeping in until he brought her a bacon, egg, and cheese from Bud's Bread Shed.

"Here you go, Onyx," Remy's mom, Amanda had chirped as she handed him three breakfast sandwiches. "You usually just get two. Remy said something about you having a new girlfriend?"

"Yeah," Onyx smiled sheepishly.

"And Madison Vine let you live?"

Apparently there were no secrets in small towns.

"No doubt she's plotting my death as we speak," Onyx admitted with an eye roll.

"Women, bleh," Bud Oliver spat.

Amanda's father-in-law and Remy's grandpa, Bud was the town cynic. If Bud was smiling and happy, you should probably run for your life because it was surely the end of days. Bud was never happy and never said anything nice, ironically, much to the delight of everyone in town.

"I can't believe anybody in their right mind would pay six got' dang dollars for a sandwich. Why in blue blazes did you name this crap hole after me, Amanda? I always told my son, that one has a screw loose. Whole dang town ain't nothing but a loony bin, payin' six dollars for a got' dang sandwich."

"Oh, Bud," Amanda cooed, refilling his coffee cup.

"That just dills my pickle. All these folks buyin' a new boat every time the old one gets wet. Money don't grow on trees, you know."

Onyx nodded his goodbyes, stuffed a dollar in the tip jar, and went to collect Ivy. When he told her about Bud's life lesson that morning, she had laughed so hard, she nearly spit out the bite she was chewing.

"Well he would be proud of me," Ivy said. "These jeans were my mom's in the eighties. I love the jalapeños on this sandwich."

She tore off another bite. Onyx gave a sideways look of approval. In his mind, Ivy got more chill with each passing day.

"So, you think there's really nothing your

dad or my parents can do about the pipeline?" Ivy asked.

They hiked through the land surrounding the creek bed where Onyx had first seen the Stone Witch. Ivy didn't tell him that she had glimpsed her on the way home from orientation about a half mile from here, where the meadow reached the forest.

"Not unless a new species is discovered," Onyx sighed. "Or a burial ground."

Ivy stopped and rolled the thought around in her head. She thought back to the Catacombs in Paris. Each society had ways of preserving and honoring the dead. Funeral customs in some cultures were mysterious to say the least.

"So, a Viking settlement, runestones seeming to mark a boundary, and no graves? Did they all just disappear?"

Ivy thought back to the Stone Witch. She had a name. Morgana. She was terrifying and breathtaking and she was surely protecting something.

"I know," Onyx shrugged.

They passed a stone statue of one of the Viking warriors in the forest. The trees had almost grown around it. Onyx pointed out the carving of a man, taller than Onyx with one long braid down his back. He held a curved axe.

"There are twelve others like this around the nature reserve, but they're all inside the runestones. They're all different. I mean, they're all stone, but they're unique."

A cold chill ran down Ivy's back. She linked her arm through Onyx's and burrowed her face into his shoulder. The stone man's eyes seemed at the same time, dead and full of dormant life.

"I don't know what will happen if the boundary is crossed. I know it's just an old legend, but I've heard that if anyone tries to take the Gray King's land as their own, the Stone Men will come alive and wage war, like they did in the old days."

Onyx sighed and passed his water bottle to Ivy. She took a drink and then a few seconds later coughed and spit out the water. Onyx thought she might be choking, but she let out a sharp bark of laughter. She doubled over, and then stood back up, her face bright red and grinning.

"What?" Onyx asked.

"Just tell them to go to the Bread Shed. Bud will put up a good fight."

Onyx tilted his head back with his own laugh.

"And Flip can sound the alarm."

"You know, we'd make a good team, put up a good fight," Ivy said, putting two tiny fists up in the air.

"Hit my arm," Onyx said, holding out a bicep.

"No! I'll hurt you," Ivy insisted.

"Do it."

"Okay, you asked for it, tough guy."

Ivy wound up her hardest punch and landed it on Onyx's bicep.

"Ow, jeez," she said, shaking out her hand. "You're the one who's stone."

Onyx smiled.

"Nah, I'm a big marshmallow. Besides, I'd protect you."

Ivy laughed, walking back to the four wheeler. She had a deadline for the paper and Onyx needed to help his mom unload a shipment for Sweet Tea and Tiffany. Ivy smiled up at her own reflection, glinting off Onyx's sunglasses. She liked who she was with him.

All seemed calm on the Gray King's land, but neither Ivy nor Onyx noticed the stone man turn his head, his eyes following the two of them all the way out of the forest.

CHAPTER 15

A Familiar Face

A few weeks later, Ivy sat up in bed, swatting for her phone. She put down House of Mirth, stopping to mark her place and debated pushing the video chat icon. Everly's impatient pout waited on the other side of the screen. It was late. They may be in different time zones, but hey, late is late.

"Heyee," Ivy answered with a forced smile.

"What's up, hoe?" Everly shouted.

She was with a bunch of their old friends in Phoenix. They were at one of the parks, drinking. The guys she was with were seniors and the girls laughed way too hard at everything they said. Everly's deep crimson lipstick was streaked and she was laughing at something imaginary. She took a drag of what Ivy hoped was a cigarette and smoke curled out of her mouth.

"I'm just headed out," Ivy lied. "Big party."

In reality her friends from the newspaper, Jacqui, Shay, and Lettie had come over to make homemade pizza. She had planned on making it alone, one of her favorite things to do with Beckett when he was still alive, but it was Shay's birthday and they invited her to watch a movie with them. Ivy was in the middle of letting the dough rise, so she offered to make Shay's birthday dinner. She already made a necklace for her and this would be the perfect time to give it to her.

"Thanks, Ivy. This is tight," Shay said when she unwrapped the glass galaxy inside the pendant. She slipped the necklace over her head, lifting her braids aside, a wide smile spreading over her face.

Her friends left after the movie was over. Ivy took a hot bubble bath with one of the candles Olivia's friend, Grace, made for her and wondered how she ever stayed out with Everly. They teetered around the Phoenix squares in heels and ridiculous party dresses, till the small hours of the morning, sneaking back in her room unnoticed.

"You better be going out!" Everly cawed. "I heard you had a new guy, too. I'm impressed."

"What?" Ivy asked.

"Yeah, you dumb skank. Your new man candy has been tagging you in all his pics."

Ivy groaned internally. Onyx always posted their pictures to his Instagram, but Ivy didn't think the tags would show up in any of her followers' feeds. She learned she was wrong. Not only was Madison insisting he was just doing it to just make her jealous, Everly had found out about her new relationship. Everly was the one person, even more than Madison, that she didn't want finding out about Onyx. Whereas Madison wanted Ivy out of the picture, Everly always wanted to be in the center of the picture. Everything was about her, and Ivy didn't want to be around her, compared to her, or influenced by her anymore. Ivy promised herself the move would be a fresh start.

Sometimes the most painful betrayals are the promises you make to yourself, and then break.

"Getting ice cream with my beautiful girlfriend?" Everly laughed, the cruel edge in her voice mocking Onyx's caption. "You're gonna be his fat piece of whale girlfriend if you keep that up. It's so cute that you think he really likes you. He's probably just parking with you until the skinny brunette makes a return."

"What?" Ivy asked, her heart rate quickening.

"Yeah, he still has pictures of his ex on his Instagram. You think I wouldn't check up on him for you? I mean, I can see why you would be stressing about it. She's class president, a varsity cheerleader, and practically a size negative zero."

Everly's right.

That nasty voice came creeping back inside Ivy's head. She told herself a thousand times that she wouldn't listen to it, but there it was, shredding at her confidence with the edges of a hundred razor blades. Still, she made herself smile. She congratulated herself for the lie she told that would end the conversation. Another opportunity presented itself when a call beeped through Everly's video chat.

"Hey, I have to get to that party. Trystan is calling."

"Another guy? Dang, Ivy. A few more and you can be on my level," Everly said. "But that will never happen, like ever. Bye, hoebag!"

Ivy sighed and hung up with Everly. Thankfully she was gone, but Trystan Crimi really was calling. Ivy wondered what he wanted. The two of them hadn't really talked since they turned in their history project.

"Hello?" Ivy answered cautiously.

"Hey, Ivy. It's Trystan. You know, from history? And biology too, I guess."

"Mmm hmm," she answered, unsure of herself.

"Well, the freshman class officers decided to have a fundraiser, a spaghetti dinner, and we were wondering if you could write something about it, in the newspaper maybe? J.D. Long, you know him? His dad broke his femur when he fell off a bull. The bull came down on it pretty hard. He's going to have a lot of medical bills. We wanted to do something for the family to help them out."

Ivy breathed out a sigh of relief.

"Sure, I'd be glad to," she answered honestly.

"Great. I can't meet after school because of football, but I can come over after I get home. You don't live very far from me," he paused. "I've seen you get off the bus a few times."

"Oh, right," Ivy said.

"Okay well, I know it's late. I'm sorry about that. I've been up watching my little brothers."

Ivy wondered if they were all as boat shoe and monogram loving as he was. Be nice, her inner voice told her. He's a nice guy and he's just trying to help. Or is he? Maybe Madison was sitting right by his side, listening in, waiting, using Trystan to trip her up.

Ivy tried to stay away from magic, but she couldn't help herself. She waved a hand over the disc of amethyst geode sitting on her nightstand. The disc crackled to life. Ivy muted her phone and whispered into the disc.

"Show me Trystan."

The image was hazy. She hadn't been practicing enough, but the image pieced together, fragmented at first, and then formed a full picture. Trystan sat at an oak desk in a very plaid bedroom. He was wearing striped pajama pants and was talking on his cell phone. He didn't have a shirt on.

"Whoa," Ivy fell back onto the mound of pillows on her bed. She waved her hand back over the image and it faded into the geode.

"Are you okay?" Trystan asked.

"Yeah. I just, um, I shocked myself," Ivy winced.

"I do that all the time. I should probably let you go. It's late."

"Okay, later."

Ivy hung up and immediately clicked open Instagram and scrolled through Onyx's profile of images. There were pictures of the two of them, a video of one of Flip's flip out moments, a few from the tournament, a few of Bailey as Martha Washington at her school play, several pictures of the nature reserve, and sure enough, if she scrolled far enough, there was Madison.

Ivy felt like throwing up. There was cheerleader Madison, one from the day she won class president, and one from the freshman formal last year. Scrolling farther, there were even more pictures of Madison. Ivy dropped her phone. Panicked, she did what she did every night, not because she wanted to see Onyx, but because she needed to know he was being honest. Ivy waved her hand over the amethyst.

"Show me Onyx."

Onyx appeared in the disc, sleeping on gray sheets with a black comforter pulled up around him. His hair was messy and his lips were curved at an odd angle from sleep.

Ivy sighed with relief, but still leaned back on her pillows, fighting tears. Of course, they won. She cried herself to sleep, waking up with puffy eyes. The next morning, her phone rang. Onyx was supposed to take her fishing.

Yeah right, you probably just want to make Madison jealous, Ivy thought bitterly.

All day she ignored his calls and texts. Several addicting visits to the disc revealed him fishing alone, reading to Bailey, and then going over film with the rest of the football team. Ivy sat on her bed with her head in her palms, wracking her brain. He told her he was finally glad to be free from Madison, but why was she all over his Instagram?

The next morning at school, a knot formed in Ivy's stomach. With each step it twisted into a nervous ball of energy. She looked up and saw Onyx's head over everyone else's. She debated on making a beeline for class, but she wanted to confront him.

"Hey," Ivy crossed her arms and gave him her best I-mean-business look.

"Hey yourself, Ive. We were supposed to go fishing yesterday. What happened to you?"

"Why didn't you just take Madison?" Ivy snapped.

"What?" Onyx asked, seeming genuinely bewildered. "What are you talking about?"

"You have tons of pictures of her on your Instagram. You must still like her, so you should probably just hang out with her."

"No I don't," Onyx shook his head. "Or if I do, they're really old and she probably hassled me so much about it that I just gave in. What's going on with you?"

Ivy sucked in a sharp breath and held it. Onyx continued.

"Do you want my passwords, Ivy? That doesn't really seem like a you sort of thing, but if you want all my passwords, you can have them. I'm not hiding anything from you. I mean, Madison used to yell at me all the time to give em' to her but whatever. If you want to act like Madison, go ahead."

"Act like Madison? I'm not crazy! You have tons of pictures of her on your Insta and you probably would like it if I acted like her because you still like her!"

Onyx laughed and shot a glance to the ceiling. He shook his head but looked back to her. Ivy was shaking, her eyes brimming with tears.

"Come on, Ive. What's going on with you? This isn't about Madison or old pictures or anything. I know there's something else. What's really bothering you?"

Ivy shook her head. Onyx's eyes were full of concern. He tried to put his arms around her but she pushed him away.

"I have to get to class," she whimpered.

Ivy stole one last look at Onyx. He was watching her walk to class. His face was familiar. He looked just like she felt.

CHAPTER 16

If I Had Known
Inksgate, 1131 A.D.

Morgana woke to muscular arms carrying her off the shore. The sky was cloudy above. She rolled her face into the fur around the collar of King Harek's massive cloak. She didn't want to scare anyone with her marred face. It was colder in the North. A shiver wracked through her body.

"I will send Arin's wife, Syrine, with warmer clothing for you," Harek said, into the air and to her.

"I will be fine. I am fine. Put me down. I just need to rest a moment, then I can do more."

Harek obeyed her orders and set Morgana lightly on the barren ground.

"Can you build a fire?" Morgana asked. "Just a small one. All I need is the ash."

Harek collected the sparse firewood they had.

"Do not hex us, Stone Witch," Harek

implored, the great warrior king's voice cracking, betraying fear and mistrust gnawing at his stomach along with intense hunger.

A small boy, not yet five years old ran past, clutching an apple in each hand, ripping chunks off the fruit, barely stopping to chew. Harek's people had been starving to death. He looked at her, ignoring him and watching the little boy, with the energy to run after he had been so hungry for so long.

"You wouldn't, would you," he whispered, more to himself than anyone.

After Harek built the fire, Morgana took the ash and mixed it with sea water. She gave bowls of the ash and saltwater to the people and instructed them to sprinkle the fields with the simple potion.

Morgana knelt, placing her palms on the earth and pulsed all the light she had into the ground, now healed from the rot that had plagued the land. Like the unrolling of a great carpet, the land unfurled over itself, revealing freshly plowed fields for miles. The new land shot up vegetables, wheat, oats, and barley, and twenty different types of herbs for medicine. Morgana felt her body growing weak.

"I can do more tomorrow, but I need to sleep."

Harek nodded.

"I will have Syrine fix a room for you in the Great Hall, next to mine. You will be safe there."

"We have been through this," Morgana disputed. "I can take care of myself."

"You choose to be alone in a village?" Harek asked.

"I choose to be alone in this life," Morgana retorted. "I will not let anyone go hungry, but I will be left alone. I do not wish to cross swords with you, King Harek."

"Harek. You may call me Harek, and since you first tore one of my finest warriors limb from limb, and flung another out to sea, I knew we were bound to cross swords."

Harek smiled a wry smile and crossed his arms. Morgana turned her back to him. The sunlight bounced off her red hair in waves. Harek could see her shoulders rise and fall with the effort of her next feat.

Morgana wicked her hand in a few cross motions, detonating a large boulder into square bricks. With a swish of her arms, the bricks sailed themselves into place, forming a modest stone structure. She then raked her hand upward. The dried grass followed her motion, erupting into the sky, and lying down on the structure, forming a thatched roof. Morgana turned back to Harek.

"You see?" she goaded. "I am perfectly capable of taking care of myself."

Harek nodded. Morgana had grown stronger every day on Holy Island. She was able to strengthen her powers to build bridges for the Priory and the village. She cleared roads for them. She grew vegetables and herbs but Harek had taken it all away in one swooping raid, the one place that felt like home. Her heart ached to think of Thomas.

Just then, the little boy ran past her feet. He was so fast, he swished the hem of her dress before running into the stone house she had just built. A wooden sword clamored at his side.

"Alfie! Wait!"

His mother ran behind him. She must be Syrine, Arin's wife. She chased him past Harek, while Arin stopped at his brother's side, looking on. The little boy ran into the small house and poked his face out the front door.

"She made us a house, Mama! The lady who came to help us made us a fine little house!"

The little boy danced in the house. He took off his wooden sword and laid it down in the center of the room. Syrine, his mother, shook her head and looked back to her husband in confusion and fear. Arin shrugged. Harek tossed his head back and laughed. It would seem that his nephew had made his first Viking conquest. A grin spread over little Alfie's small, dirty face as he ran, belting out a yip of a roar.

The boy ran to Morgana, tugging on her skirts. She knelt down, surprised at the misty tears beginning to spill from her eyes.

"Do I frighten you, child?" Morgana asked.

"No," Alfie answered simply, running his tiny hands over her face and hair. "You made my family the most wonderful little house. I am glad to know you, Lady Morgana."

Morgana smiled as the salty tears spilled down her cheeks. She pulled Alfie into a hug, her first since the day Father Thomas rescued her from the beach.

"Enjoy your most wonderful house then, sweet boy," Morgana said. "May you and your family have much love and happiness there."

Morgana rose, leaving Alfie to explore the house she had built for herself, which he claimed for his family. He isn't so different from his uncle, Morgana thought as she watched the people of Inksgate pull cabbages from the ground, cooking and eating their first meals in days. They fed the young and the old first, then ate as happily as only the hungry can. Morgana nodded to Harek.

"I will thank you to show me to my room in the Great Hall."

In the summer months that followed, Morgana grew accustomed to the Viking ways of life, but she hadn't grown accustomed to the drafty Great Hall. The warm summer breezes were fine, but she decided to build Harek another hall, a Winter Hall. She had been working on her masonry and knew she could lay the stones perfectly.

Syrine and her servant girls helped sew new Viking clothes for her and they helped her braid her long, red hair so that the winds from the ocean wouldn't whip it into a tangled frenzy. Some of them were afraid to touch it, all of them being shades of blonde.

Harek was mostly gray haired, though his face was young. Morgana watched him as he ran his hands over the tall wheat stalks in the field. She watched him training, his thick, dark brows knitting together in concentration. He was an expert with many different kinds of weapons and continued to invent new ones. He drew pictures on skins in animal blood or charcoal for his blacksmith who had nearly died in the famine. Morgana watched him test a new curved axe one day.

"I could do that," she said.

"Could you?" Harek asked, amused. "You're intolerant to iron. What do you think this is made of?"

"The handle is wood, you donkey's rear."

Harek stared at her. He was a confusing, maddening man. He was the most brutal warlord anyone had ever seen. He could kill you ten ways before you hit the ground and yet he played gently with his nephew and made the rounds every morning to check on the old and the sick. He left broth and bread outside her door when the magic left her depleted. Morgana watched him scoop up a palmful of grass one day, rubbing the blades together and inhaling the scent of the earth, the land itself. She found herself thinking about him often and watched him while he trained.

The trees had begun to grow back in Inksgate. Once they reached maturity a few weeks later, Morgana cut them down with a swish of her cloak and flew them over to the top of her favorite hill. New trees began to sprout immediately.

When the moon grew full, Morgana stood on top of the hill and pulsed her stone magic through her feet, carving out the hillside. She worked the stones and timber around the hillside, forming the largest structure in Inksgate. She designed it after the Priory, the most beautiful place she had ever seen. She lined the hall with the freshly cut timber. She fashioned long tables for everyone in Inksgate and a large fire pit in the center. Finally, she sailed a large boulder into the hall and there, in Harek's Winter Hall, she carved a giant throne into being from one solid piece of rock. Then, darkness overcame her. She had fallen over, exhausted.

She woke up to a vice grip on both of her arms.

Harek stood over her. They were alone.

"You did this for me, for Inksgate?"

Morgana nodded. Then, she smiled.

"My room is over there," she pointed.

Harek nodded and laughed. She designed a hot spring below the hall and hollowed out the walls of her room to run hot water through the stones for warmth. The cold never suited her. It never suited her mother either.

"I never told you how sorry I am for your arrival in Inksgate," Harek swallowed and gazed at the fresh floorboards. "When I heard there was a sorceress who could help us, who could save us, I had to find her and bring her here. I would die for my land, my people, my home, but I am so sorry that you came to Inksgate in chains. I will never forgive myself. If I had known-"

"Stop, Harek. Please," Morgana put a single finger over his lips, dragging it down so only his bottom lip rested below her index finger. "You didn't know. I saw how they were. I saw for myself. I couldn't stand by and do nothing. Neither could you."

Harek nodded.

"If I don't die a warrior, if I am not killed in battle, I will never enter Valhalla," Harek began, sucking in a wavering breath while watching Morgana's chin begin to tremble. "You have given me something to fight for. You have given me my home back, to defend. A king is nothing without his kingdom. I do not wish to rule over bodies and ashes. You have given me my kingdom back. You have given me myself back. I hope, in time, the kingdom could be yours as well. I hope that with time, I could be yours."

Harek took her hand.

"Wait here," he asked.

Morgana watched Harek jog to the woodshed down the hill. He stole one last glance at her before he entered.

He emerged carrying a massive, wooden throne. It had to weigh as much as two of his warriors combined. Harek hoisted the throne over his shoulder and hiked up the steep hill to the hall. As he approached, Morgana could see that the throne was solid oak, carved with flowers, vines, feathers, waves, the sun, moon, and stars. All the beautiful elements that made Inksgate the paradise that it was.

Harek carried the throne into the hall and swung it down next to his stone throne. It was smaller, not made for him. It was made for a queen. He took a breath, steadying himself. He held out a calloused, battle worn hand. Morgana took it, cautiously at first.

The thoughts in her head seemed to rush like the current over the river rocks, but the warm roughness of Harek's hand steadied her.

"Forgive me," she whispered. "I am sorry, Harek. I am haunted by my actions and if I had known-"

"But you did not," he finished.

Morgana used Harek's outstretched hand to pull herself into his arms. He tilted his face toward her, flawed with a few of his own scars. He ran his hand along her marked cheek.

"You are the most exquisite girl I have ever laid my eyes upon," Harek confessed.

"You are not frightened?" she asked.

"I am. I am terrified," Harek answered. "Only now. Only because I have so much to lose. I am not scared of you. I am scared of being without you."

Morgana wrapped her hands around

Harek's neck and kissed him. She knew they were both scared, but with one healing kiss, as the sea kisses the sky, Morgana forgave the past and forgave herself, creeping second by second into the future with the warrior king who considered her the fiercest warrior of them all.

CHAPTER 17

Playing Games

Ivy avoided Onyx. She avoided looking at anything online and for once, she asked Jacqui to cover for her at the game. She didn't think she could handle watching Madison cheering for Onyx on the sidelines. What would her headline read? "Chubby Nerd Stupidly Falls for Football Star Who Still Has Thing for Cheerleader Ex?" That would make the front page.

"Ivy, come on," Jacqui said, running a hand through silver and purple hair. "This is dumb. The pictures on his Insta are all of her by herself. That's thick. Who does that? Say that out loud to yourself, okay Ivy?"

"I don't want to think about it," Ivy huffed.

I don't want to think about Onyx, or Beckett, or my mom, or anything.

"I don't want to watch Wheel of Fortune with Meemaw every night, but it's the only way to get her to take her pills," Jacqui said with her hands on her hips. "And she lives with us because she got kicked out of the home, so that's my life right now. Here we are. This is reality."

Jacqui was making sense, but it still didn't add up to her.

Still, Ivy's spirits lifted the tiniest bit. The fair was in town. Ivy went with Jacqui, Lettie, and Shay. They rode all the rides and went overboard on corn dogs and fried candy bars.

Ivy was wrist deep in a bag of cotton candy when Onyx rounded the corner with Flip, D'Mario, Remy, and Caleb. She spotted Flip first, jumping around with an inflatable hammer he had just won. He was bashing D'Mario over the head with it, a little squeaky sound bleating out with each air-filled wallop. D'Mario was about to grab the hammer, but rethought his strategy and calmly paid to play a shooting game. He won a large foam cowboy hat that offset the hammer blows. All was right with the world.

Ivy watched them for a bit and then ducked behind the cheese curd truck as soon as Onyx looked her way. He waved to her friends.

"Hey!" he called. "Is Ivy with you guys?"

"Yeah she's right-"

Lettie cut herself off when Jacqui cleared her throat loud enough to startle the very large man hitting a hammer on a springboard. The weight flew a few feet up and then came crashing down. Jacqui ignored his dirty look.

"She's with us in spirit," Jacqui nodded, pressing her palms together as if she were in prayer.

Lettie shot a confused look and then caught on. She nodded along with Jacqui and Shay.

"Right," Onyx said. "How's your Meemaw? I heard she got kicked out of Shady Pines for brewing toilet wine."

"Every family's got one, Onyx," Jacqui replied, rolling her eyes. "And it was the bedpans, not the toilet."

He gave her a half smile, checked his phone, and adjusted his black baseball cap. Always black with a black Texas Rangers logo.

"You look nice tonight, Lettie," D'Mario said, tipping his comically large, green foam cowboy hat.

"Thanks," she giggled.

Onyx nodded his thanks to all of them. He continued down the midway, following Flip and D'Mario in their war of blow-up hammer versus foam cowboy hat. Remy added the light-up blinky sword to the mix and the war raged on.

"Why don't you just talk to him?" Lettie fussed. "Does he look like he still likes Madison? She's coming this way from the events pavilion, probably stalking him."

Lettie pointed at a very determined looking Madison, stalking down the midway. She glanced around and stomped off toward the other rides.

"How do you know that they didn't come together?" Ivy asked.

"Because Remy can only fit five in his car.

It's a Maxima," Lettie retorted with a shake of her head. "Now clap back to that."

Ivy sighed and stuffed another handful of blue sugary cotton candy into her mouth.

"I can't even right now," Ivy said.

"She can't even, y'all!" Shay hooted.

The girls dissolved into giggles and picked up another order of fried Oreos.

Trystan came over the next day to talk about the article. He didn't have time to stay, so they made plans to talk about the dinner at the fair the next night. Trystan had to go to the fair. His mom was winning a prize for her cheesecake.

"I can't miss it, so you might as well come," Trystan said with a shrug. "It's the only night I have free because of football and church, but Mom won first prize, so I have to go watch her. She was so excited. She never wins anything."

"But I went two days ago," Ivy shrugged.

The fair food was probably clobbering her stomach but Trystan said lots of people go more than once, so Ivy nodded in agreement. She was happy that Trystan was happy and agreed to meet him at the fair. When she told her parents, they said they would come check it out, so it seemed pretty logical. Max Jasper needed to look at the mowers anyhow, and there was no better place for mowers and hot tubs than the fair.

So, while Sarah Crimi accepted her award for Best Overall Dessert in Show, Ivy and Trystan strolled the midway, talking about the dinner. They planned to pick up the food, set up the tables around the gazebo in the middle of town, and clean up afterward. Trystan had the schedules and sign up sheets ready to be printed. Ivy had a few tweaks to the article to make, but for the most part, it was ready to go.

"I'm just gonna stop real quick," Ivy said, passing the fried Oreo stand. "I mean, YOLO, right?"

"Yeah," Trystan laughed. "You do only live once."

He stopped by the milk jug game.

"That's rigged," Ivy said. "They're too heavy, so there's no way to win."

"Nah," Trystan said. "You have to have faith. Besides, you just have to hit it in the middle. Let's test the old throwing arm."

Trystan wound up, threw the ball, and knocked the cans off in one long swoop, hitting the cans where they met in the middle, using expert precision. The man running the booth nodded and handed Trystan a large stuffed banana.

"Nice prize," Ivy laughed.

"You think so?" Trystan asked, raising his eyebrows.

"No," Ivy replied. "It's kind of dumb."

"The game is dumb. It's a ball and some old cans, but that's the fun of it," Trystan laughed, handing the banana to a little girl who seemed to be admiring it. The banana was wearing sunglasses.

"Play dumb games, win dumb prizes," Ivy mused.

"Yep," Trystan replied. "Which is why I don't play games."

"But you just did!" Ivy countered.

"You know what I mean," Trystan said, putting his hands in his pockets and strolling back to the main pavilion.

Ivy knew what he meant. It was pretty good advice. It was easier said than done. Sometimes it was hard to recognize a player in a game you didn't know existed, with rules you'd never understand.

The Long family desperately needed help with Jerrett Long's medical bills and they were so grateful that Trystan and the freshman officers had the dinner plans coordinated. Trystan said he couldn't just stand by. J.D. was one of his best friends.

The local Italian restaurant, Meatballs, donated plenty of spaghetti and meat sauce. Wayne and Amanda Oliver, Remy's parents, donated salad and homemade breadsticks from Bud's Bread Shed.

The night of the dinner, Trystan asked if Ivy minded to pick up the salad and breadsticks. The sophomore class pitched in to help and organized a talent show for the entertainment. It was pretty much just Madison trying to sing a bad pop song, but whatever, Ivy thought. Either way, with the sophomore class helping, they had a few cars to get from place to place.

"Mom has everything ready," Remy said after he picked up Ivy.

When they entered the Bread Shed, Bud was slumped over, sleeping at a table with two coffee cups and a half eaten bagel in front of him. The customers mulled around him, used to and maybe fond of, his presence. Remy went back to get the baskets of bread and when he slammed the doors to the kitchen, Bud perked awake.

"Can't a poor old man get any sleep around here?"

Bud yelled to the back of the shop, but no one was listening.

"I said! Can't the elderly get any got' dang rest around here!"

"I thought coffee was supposed to wake you up," Ivy said, pointing to the two coffee cups in front of Bud.

"Only one of em's coffee," he snarked. "Are you that girl the big boy likes? The one with the weird name?"

"Onyx?" Ivy asked, surprised, but yet not really surprised that Bud had a handle on the town gossip.

"That's the one. I don't know why these parents try to get all fancy with the names. Kids these days. They all wanna be special and different. What happened to just getting a job? Now they think everyone needs to know your opinion. Y'all got enough mouth for two sets o' teeth."

"I don't think he likes me," Ivy shrugged.

"Most o' them boys is dumber than a fence post and just as ugly. If he don't like you, just move on," Bud's eye began to twinkle. "But I wouldn't say that's the case."

"I think he still likes Madison," Ivy shrugged. "And I know you know who she is. Everyone does."

"The Vine girl? Yep, I know the one. Comes in here and always complains that everything has too many carbs. What the red barn on fire is a carb? She seems to like the smell of her own cow patties a little too much, if you ask me. And she's slicker than thin grease on a hot griddle. You watch her."

"What do you mean?" Ivy asked.

"It's just what I hear," Bud said, not really answering the question.

He snuffled and adjusted himself in the booth before falling back asleep.

"You ready?" Remy asked.

Ivy nodded and grabbed the bags of bread while Remy hauled the salad out to the car. They sat in silence since Remy's stereo was broken.

"Onyx is going to be there, just telling you," Remy warned.

"I know," Ivy sighed.

At the dinner that night, Madison was

getting ready for her singing debut. She was wearing a black and white striped dress, the same dress she was wearing in one of the pictures on Onyx's Instagram. She smiled and jutted her shoulder out, turning her chin to pose as everyone walked past. One of the other cheerleaders stopped to gush over Madison's dress.

"Thanks! I bought it last week! It's brand new. I'd never wear anything on sale," Madison said.

Wait, Ivy thought. Last week?

She clicked her phone open and scrolled through Onyx's page. The caption under the picture of her wearing the striped dress read "Madison looking so gorgeous on a most amazing June day". It was October. Something wasn't adding up.

Ivy frantically saved the pictures and texted them to Caleb.

-Can you tell when these pictures were taken?

It didn't take long for Caleb to work his magic.

-All of these were taken 9 days ago and uploaded 8 days ago. The geotag is from Big Cabin.

Onyx was in Muskogee for an away game eight days ago, Ivy thought to herself. He always reviews film on his iPad before games and sleeps on the bus. There was no way he would have time to take ten different pictures of Madison, just Madison, in ten different outfits and post them. Something wasn't adding up.

Just then, she felt a tap on her shoulder.

"Hey," Madison Vine cooed in a soft voice. "I think you might want this. Onyx left it at my house last night. He was there really late."

Madison pouted her lips, and shoved a black baseball cap into her hands. A few days ago, Ivy would have dropped the cap and ran to bathroom in tears, but she wasn't falling for it.

"Thanks," Ivy said. "I can return this and get him one he would actually wear."

"What? This is his," Madison insisted.

"Then why is it a Cardinals hat?" Ivy asked. "He's a Rangers fan."

"He went to St. Louis with his dad this summer. Didn't he tell you?" Madison asked, a hint of triumph seeping through.

"Yeah, to watch the Rangers. Besides, the logo isn't black. He always wears a black logo on a black hat. Cowboys, Thunder, or Rangers, it's always a black logo."

"What? I-"

Madison hesitated, but Ivy kept going.

"And the sticker is still on the bottom of the brim. He takes those off and puts them on his locker. Have you seen his locker? It's covered in New Era stickers. That's not even a New Era hat. And just so you know, Caleb is changing Onyx's passwords so you can't spam his social media anymore. I'm adding that little anecdote to my article about online safety and privacy."

All the color drained out of Madison's face.

"Sorry Madison. Play stupid games, win stupid prizes."

Ivy took the hat, added it to the silent auction table, and walked off to go serve spaghetti.

CHAPTER 18

SEE FOR YOURSELF

Onyx looked over his dad's shoulder at the scatter plot on the computer. He was using some of his dad's test data on the birds from the park for a math project. Jay Rainwater had measured the amount of nests per square mile in parts of the park. He was still looking for the mythic salt crane. The bird was almost a cryptid, a mythical creature, like Bigfoot. Everyone knew it was out there, but no one had any proof. Onyx was finding patterns within the numbers when a loud voice startled him.

"Hey man! It's the On-Bomb. Big Ox, what's happening?"

Harbor was already grinning and leaning over the desk for a high five. Onyx smiled and shook his head. He wasn't leaving Harbor hanging.

"Hey Harbor, to what do we owe this momentous occasion?" Jay asked.

Everyone in the family was fond of Harbor.

Tiffany had let him in. He already had an Eskimo Joe's cup of sweet tea sweating in his hand.

"No occasion, I came down with Olivia. She's at Ivy's. I stole Ivy's bike and came over to show my ugly mug, see how everyone was doing."

"Awe, what a cute little yellow bicycle with a basket and a little bell!" Tiffany called into the study.

"Yeah, I stole it, and I dinged that bell all the way here. Listen, Ivy and Olivia are headed to the forest. I just wanted to let you know. That, and I'm sorry I spanked you so bad in Call of Duty last night."

"No you're not," Onyx said.

"No, I'm not, but Sugar and Spice are totally headed into the spooky old forest, just so you know."

Onyx was already putting on his shoes.

"I can't believe you have your driver's license," Ivy said, seeming almost bewildered that Olivia was driving them to the forest on the nature reserve in her new deep purple Mini Cooper.

"I know, I mean, being able to drive yourself around," Olivia smiled. "It's almost like magic."

Ivy laughed at the irony. The girls parked the car and hiked through the meadow to the edge of the forest. Ivy pointed to the tree line.

"Do you know about the Stone Witch?" Ivy asked.

Olivia nodded. She had seen. The magic

Olivia tried so hard to avoid eventually broke through in a watershed moment when Harbor was about to jump off a bluff in Keystone Lake. The guys went bluff jumping all the time, but right before he jumped, an image of a sunken boat flooded into Olivia's mind. The image blurred to one of Harbor's body, floating in a pool of his own blood. If he jumped off the bluff, he would hit the sunken boat just below the surface and be killed. Harbor didn't hear her until was too late. He had already jumped.

Olivia immediately flooded the lake with all the water she could conjure and raised the water level almost five feet. Olivia then pulled him up to safety on a wave so large that it covered the side of the bluff.

The water receded out to the rest of the lake, revealing the mangled, sunken boat. No one knew how it had gotten there, but it hadn't been there long.

"At least we were alone," Olivia surmised. "If anything had happened to him, I don't know what I would do."

"He's the one then, huh?" Ivy mused.

"He's always been the one," Olivia admitted, a smile hiding the moisture at the corners of her eyes. She switched the subject. "So, why didn't you call Ashley?"

"Why do you think?" Ivy shrieked, swatting at her cousin.

"Hey, she's faced down a ghost and lived to tell about it, too."

"No way," Ivy replied. "She thinks she knows everything. You can see the future and you still don't act like you know everything."

"Fire witches run hot," Olivia shrugged. "And stone witches are hard to move and even harder to crack. And sometimes, people change, so the future changes."

Ivy stood in the meadow letting Olivia's words sink in. No matter how big the stone, it will always be worn down by water in the end. It just takes a little while. The girls startled as the low rumble of an engine approached.

"Sorry Ivy," Olivia shrugged. "We've got company."

CHAPTER 19

HERE COMES THE BRIDE
INKSGATE, 1132 A.D.

The hem of Morgana's rich teal gown swept the floor of the Winter Hall as she paced toward the flames in the fire pit directly in front of Harek's throne. He was having a feast for Inksgate. The entire village was gathered in the hall. Wine, mead, and roasted geese made their rounds along with rich vegetable stews and chewy, browned bread. Poached pears swam in sticky sauces, thick with spices and herbed goat's cheese adorned platters with apricots and figs.

Morgana had made a Viking version of her mother's Scottish shortbread for the feast. She kneaded butter and honey into buckwheat flour with only a few sad tears falling into the dough. She missed her mother and wished she were here in Inksgate.

Harek took a square of shortbread, handing it to Alfie, who was too small to reach the platter, but his own plate and goblet remained empty. He was waiting for her to eat.

His eyes widened when he saw her across the fire. Syrine helped her braid her long, wavy hair and line her eyes. The two of them dyed a length of fabric a deep blue, like the waters of the ocean and sewed Morgana a dress with long bell sleeves and a deep cowl hood she could raise whenever she didn't want to show her face. She had the blacksmith fashion her a bronzed chain belt. Finally, she made a necklace and earrings for both her and Syrine out of the moonstones she found while clearing the hillside for the Winter Hall. The moonstones glowed pearlescent in her ears under her red hair.

Harek extended his hand in silence. Words failed him. Morgana bowed and took his hand. That hand has brought death to thousands, Morgana thought. She took it anyhow. *And life to the ones who call him king,* echoed the other part of her mind. As she took her place on the throne next to Harek, she knew it was the part of her that was surely becoming Viking with each passing day.

In the weeks before the feast, Morgana interrupted Harek in his training pit by sailing an axe into the wooden post he was using for practice. He landed crushing blows with his massive longsword. He could almost take a swipe and cut halfway through the post. Tossing the sword aside, he unstuck the axe and flung it out of the pit.

"I did that by myself. I used no magic," she announced.

"No one interrupts me when I am training," Harek said, swiping his face on the sleeve of his sweat-soaked tunic. "Unless you are queen. Have you considered my proposal?"

"I do not have a dowry," Morgana countered.

She took in his muscular forearms, broad shoulders, and set jaw with a hint of a smile. She tossed him an apple.

"You do not need one," he insisted, taking a bite.

"But I will have one," Morgana hinted. "I just have to leave Inksgate for the night."

"You are forbidden," Harek said. "It is too dangerous. Jarl Grimstad, my sworn enemy, he will stop at nothing to take my lands and everything I hold dear. He is waiting out there, I know this."

"It is a full moon, Harek."

"Then you will stay in the Winter Hall with me on this full moon night," Harek insisted.

"Do not make me a prisoner in the hall that I built for you," Morgana glared.

"You do not understand. I will not loose you," Harek bellowed. "I have waited a lifetime for you."

"Then trust me," Morgana implored him. "I am taking Syrine with me. She has already asked Arin."

"Oh she has, has she?" Harek shot a death stare at Arin, sword fighting with another warrior a few yards away.

Arin looked away.

"Does no one tell me anything in my own kingdom?" Harek howled.

"You said you hoped I would come to think of it as my kingdom as well," Morgana reminded him.

Harek shook his head. He pulled her to him, casting aside his heavy longsword. Taking her face in his hands he kissed her, tilting his nose to the side of her cheek, deepening the kiss. He pulled away as he made up his mind.

"Go if you must, but return to me," Harek said.

"There isn't anywhere I would rather be," Morgana said, with sincere honesty. "Not in Inksgate, but with you."

Harek nodded, his words failing him once more.

"Do you fear my capture?" Morgana asked.

"No," Harek answered, then hesitated. "Yes, I do, but you are so maddening, your captors would give you back. They would kiss you a thousand times, and then give you back."

That night, Morgana and Syrine rode the last remaining horses left in the village to the cliff. Harek may have thought he knew every inch of his kingdom, but he was about to add a few more.

To get a better view of Inksgate, one day, Morgana levitated to the top of the cliffs marking the boundary. On the other side of the cliffs, on a grassy plain, grazed a herd of wild horses. She knew Harek could add them to the stables that sat empty by the Great Hall. During the great famine, all but two of the horses had died or had been eaten. If Jarl Grimstad planned to attack, they would need more horses.

Morgana whispered to Syrine to take their own horses and hide behind the rocks. She placed a palm on the rock wall, inhaling its magic, then floated herself to the top of the cliff. The herd was still grazing, some of the horses lapping at the stream running through the meadow.

Morgana grabbed a handful of grass, sparsely growing on top of the bluff. She rubbed it between her hands and exhaled the old Druid spell.

`Hursa-ros..`

The entire herd of feral horses turned to look at her. All at once, in unison, the beasts bowed, regally, to the girl who in a few days would become queen of Inksgate. Morgana forced her hands through the rock, growing her limbs, digging down into the bedrock of the earth. Then, as if she were floating a toy boat over water, she floated the cliff over the plain, unfurling the river into a great waterfall, crashing over the side of the cliff. The cliff wall came down to the earth with a shattering quake behind the horses, sending them running down the hill directly to Inksgate.

Syrine was waiting with her own horse. She rode frantically down the hill to head off the other horses. Once the stallions had calmed down from the quake, Morgana glided down the side of the cliff. She found her own horse, Harek's fasted steed.

Morgana quickly mowed down a ridge of timber by the bluffs. She had been saving it for the fence. Splitting the timber in two and working quickly, she fenced the horses in until the saddler could get to them.

As the sun rose, Morgana and Syrine rode back to find Harek pacing the hall and Arin slumped over at one of the long tables, sleeping. There was a sausage in front of Arin, so Syrine grabbed it, claiming it for her breakfast.

"He won't mind," she smiled, leaving him a potato in its place.

"I have returned," Morgana announced.

"You are home. There is a difference," Harek said, running to inspect Morgana for damage.

She was covered in dirt, but well and incredibly happy. Not only did she have a bride price of two hundred and seven horses, she had uncovered an ancient bronze age sword by moving the cliff. She would have a dowry and the customary sword for the wedding ceremony. She smiled knowing Harek was right. From the moment they first met, they were destined to cross swords. At the time, she didn't know that it was traditional in Viking wedding ceremonies to do so.

On her wedding day, Morgana rose before the sun. She would marry Harek at dawn. Syrine helped her bathe and dress in her ivory wedding gown, symbolically washing away her life before Harek. Her face remained marked, but her spirit felt clean and new. She felt as though she were never Scottish. Never a Highlander, never one of Forlan's subjects, never the object of Tiernan's selfish and twisted affections. She was always Viking and soon she would be queen.

"You never wanted to be queen?" Morgana asked Syrine as she braided flowers into her red hair for the ceremony.

"No," Syrine answered. "I never did."

She stood up, pushing her own hair aside. When she untied her tunic and revealed her back, Morgana gasped, recoiling in a unique combination of horror and pity. Deep scars criss-crossed Syrine's back. Some marks were raised, and some were indented, from pieces of skin that had been whipped off her back.

"How? When?" Morgana stuttered.

"Harek wasn't always king. Jarl Grimstad used to rule Inksgate. He was cruel, a horrible man. Did I ever tell you where I am from?"

Morgana shook her head, no. She assumed Syrine was Viking, like everyone else.

"I am from Francia. My village was raided

by Jarl Grimstad. Harek raids, but not like Grimstad. Jarl Grimstad burned my village to the ground and killed everyone I loved. He took me as a slave. Grimstad treated his dogs better than he treated his slaves. One day, I overcooked one of his kills and he had me whipped half to death. That was the day Harek and Arin's clan rose up to fight Jarl Grimstad. Arin is older than Harek. He should have rightfully battled Grimstad for the kingdom, but he passed the battle to Harek, not because he didn't want to battle, but because he saw me tied to the whipping post, bloody and inches from death. He saved me. He brought me to his mother who treated my wounds and nursed me back to health. From that day, I could only see his face, my hero. Arin chose me over being king. Harek won the battle and exiled Grimstad instead of killing him and now he is king."

"I am deeply sorry," Morgana started, but Syrine held up a hand.

"Do not be. I love my husband and son. I have a life I never dreamed of, and thanks to you, last night I was able to give Arin a stallion, my own bride price. Slaves have no dowries, but now I do."

Morgana rushed to hug Syrine. She pulled her close.

"One more thing," Syrine whispered. "Harek told Arin once he would never marry unless he was prepared to give up his kingdom, just as Arin had done for me. I knew when he began carving your throne that he had found the one. The funny thing is, you gave him back his kingdom."

Morgana sighed. Syrine finished with her hair and walked her down the dock to the edge of the ocean where she first entered Inksgate a prisoner. Harek promised he would never take her magic by force, nor would he condemn her for her powers and he kept his word.

He stood at the end of the dock, dressed in gray, the cloak around his shoulders lined with fox fur. A bronze crown adorned his head, matching a smaller, delicate silver crown, resting on a pillow in Alfie's little hands.

A Viking priestess presided over the ceremony. Morgana laid her hand on top of Harek's while the priestess bound them with a ribbon of pure crimson, the same color as the sun rising over the ocean. As she bound their hands together, Morgana and Harek vowed to love, honor, and fight for each other until the days of their deaths. Arin and Syrine crossed Harek and Morgana's chosen swords, each bearing a golden ring. With their hands still bound, they slid the rings into place. The priestess pronounced them as one and Harek placed the crown on Morgana's head, pronouncing her queen of Inksgate.

Harek leaned in to kiss her, and Morgana wrapped her unbound hand around his neck, pressing her lips to his. She ignored the cheers of the crowd, closing her eyes. She was queen now, and that meant she could do as she pleased and all she wanted to do was kiss her new husband.

As they parted, a hawk swooped down, snatching a flower from Morgana's hair. It dropped a scroll at Harek's feet. The hawk screeched at Harek and with one last flap of its wings, it flew back over the mountains.

Arin picked up the scroll. His face went white. Harek fell silent.

"What does it say?" Morgana demanded.

Arin cleared his throat.

King Harek, how kind and stupid of you to leave me alive. I write to you in good spirits. I have raised an army and I will be taking back my kingdom, along with your newest prize, the Stone Witch. Warm Regards, Jarl Grimstad.

Morgana shook her head. Maybe she was a witch, but she was also queen and no one was going to take her husband's kingdom and live. Maybe Harek had left him alive, but Morgana would not be kind or stupid enough do the same.

CHAPTER 20

A WARNING

Onyx swung himself out of the truck. He hopped over the fence leading to the meadow in one swoop, landing softly on the grass. Ivy and Olivia spun around.

"We've been through this, Onyx. You don't have a license," Ivy shouted.

"Well, I do," Harbor shouted back, giving Ivy a salute.

"No you don't," Olivia replied. "You failed your test twice."

"No one told me I couldn't eat onion rings during the test."

"And the second time?" Olivia prodded.

"That was Kai's fault, because he didn't tie the wakeboard on top of the car the right way and it came off in the middle of the street. That's not my fault, babe. Don't put that on me."

"Will both of you shut up?" Ivy huffed. "I'm sorry, it's just- why are you here?"

Onyx stuffed his hands in his pockets and

looked at the ground. Harbor took a big swig of the soda he was drinking. Onyx cleared his throat and finally broke the silence.

"I'm worried about you. The pipeline has already started and they're about to move into the forest. Some of the trees have already been cut down, see?"

Onyx pointed to the trees that had been cleared. Upon closer inspection, they oozed a black sap that seemed unnatural. The stumps they left behind had started to gray. Ivy walked closer and bent down to touch one. It was cool to the touch in the warm October sun.

"The trees have been blighted," Olivia said.

"I'm sorry- blighted?" Onyx asked, frowning.

"It means cursed, but cursed, like made unusable to anyone else but the one who cursed them. If anyone tried to use these trees for timber, they would crumble into ash. No one can take anything from this land without it falling apart," Olivia turned to look at Ivy. "I've been reading some of Grandma Cynthia's books in her attic. Mom and I are trying to make sense of them."

Onyx thought back to the time he found an interesting rock in the forest. He put it in his pocket to bring home for Bailey, but when he got home, there was only sand in his pocket. A familiar swish of black fabric snapped him out of the memory.

"I think we should go," Onyx said. He reached for Ivy's hand. "Can I talk to you?"

Ivy nodded. Olivia breathed out a slow breath, exhaling in Ivy's direction.

"Switch cars?" Ivy asked to Olivia and Harbor.

Olivia nodded and they all turned to leave. Onyx wrapped an arm around Ivy's shoulders.

"You know Madison hacked my account, right? I would never do anything to hurt you," he said.

"I know," Ivy returned. "I knew. I figured it out. I just didn't know how to tell you."

Onyx nodded.

"I knew you'd come around. You just had to see for yourself."

Just as they were making their way to the cars, a low rumble shook the ground. As they turned around, a black shape took form, rising high above the trees. Darkness fell as the shape blocked out the sun. It was the Stone Witch. Her black cloak was in tatters, but it streaked out, wispy and streaming over the forest. Her eyes were dark, her lips a deep purple, and her face bore the swirling black marks that had been cut so long ago. Her ragged hair fell in waves out of her hood. The temperature dropped at least twenty degrees.

Onyx grabbed Ivy. Harbor instinctively put himself between Olivia and the witch, but Olivia stepped in front of him. She cast low waves of blue light from the tips of her fingers, in an attempt to keep the Stone Witch at bay. The Stone Witch turned to her and with one glance, Olivia and Harbor were both blasted backward, sailing toward the road. Olivia hit the fencepost and Harbor crashed into the wire fence. He fell forward on the ground, red lines forming on his back where the wire fence had cut into him. Olivia blinked her eyes open, hazy from hitting the wooden post.

"What do you want?" she croaked.

When the Stone Witch spoke, her voice was ancient. Her words sounded in the air and in their bones.

"Do not use your magic on me, young water witch. You will find no victories here. This is the Gray King's land and all those who try to take it from him will be killed. If the usurpers are not banished by the next full moon, the Stone Men will rise and fight once again. Mark my words."

Ivy rose to her feet. Onyx tried to hold her back, but she shook him off.

"Morgana!" Ivy shouted.

The Stone Witch turned to look at her. The dark form lowered from the sky, sailing over the meadow toward Ivy. Clouds covered the sky and thunder began to roll, menacing in the sky.

"Tell us how to make them leave. Let us help you," Ivy shouted.

Ivy placed her palm to the ground and shook the earth. Morgana took a step back.

"You cannot help me," she hissed. "These are Harek's lands and they will be protected."

"He isn't here!" Ivy shouted. "There isn't anyone buried on these lands. If we found a burial ground, we could keep the pipeline away, but there isn't one. There are no bodies!"

"Oh, there are bodies, young witch," Morgana cackled. "But first, you must know where to look."

With a blast that sent them all reeling backward, the Stone Witch receded into the forest, taking the storm with her. Harbor sat up and scratched his back. The wounds were healed.

"Did you do that?" Olivia asked.

Ivy shook her head, no.

The Stone Witch had healed Harbor's wounds before she retreated back into the dark forest.

CHAPTER 21

All Hallows' Eve

Ivy glanced down at her phone in panic. It was Halloween and she was scared for good reason. Everly was coming to town. The pipeline was scheduled to cross into the forest on Monday, but it was Saturday night, Halloween, and Everly invited herself to crash Remy's Halloween party. Ivy would have to worry about the Stone Witch and the next full moon. For now, she had a different kind of monster to deal with.

Ivy thought back to the Stone Witch often, but had been too scared to go back to the forest. Now she had to face what was in front of her. The doorbell rang.

"What is that?" Everly asked, wrinkling her nose at Ivy's costume.

Tiffany Rainwater had spent days designing the silver and black sequined flapper girl dress to match Onyx's old school gangster costume. His suit was black, pinstriped with gray with a red boutonnière to match the red feather in Ivy's hair.

She wore it pulled into a low side bun. Tiffany even handmade a long string of gray pearls to match.

"I'm a flapper," Ivy offered, taking in Everly's outfit, if you could call it that.

Everly was wearing basically underwear, bunny ears, a tiny bowtie, and a fluffy white bunny tail that was larger than the rest of her outfit combined. She had lots of body glitter going on.

"Right," Everly rolled her eyes. "Let's go."

Flip picked them up in his Bronco to head out to The Swamp, where Remy had set up for the bonfire. Ivy darted out the door to meet Onyx. She couldn't help but smile at how cute he was as a mobster. His dark hair was slicked back and Ivy found herself really wishing it was the twenties. Maybe then Everly would be hauled off to the clink for indecency or lunacy or something.

"I'm not getting in that," Everly wrinkled her nose. "Not with that guy."

"What?" Flip asked, taking off his scary clown mask. "You have a cake to pop out of or something?"

"Let's go. They have alcohol," Ivy placated, a trick that always worked back in Phoenix.

"Fine," Everly huffed.

Walking to The Swamp wasn't bad, but Everly complained the whole way. That is, until Remy came to greet them. He jogged up the hill in a referee costume, tooting a whistle.

"Whoa!" he called, landing cartoon wolf popping eyes on Everly. "Violation! You are too hot to enter. Penalty box is next to me, ma'am. Let's go."

"I can't. My heels," Everly smiled, batting long, fake eyelashes.

Remy obliged, carrying Everly off and setting her on one of the picnic tables around the bonfire. He promised to return with spiked punch. Ivy blew out the breath she had been holding in and reminded herself to steal some whisky for Remy.

"Thanks Ivy," he winked with two cups full of mystery punch.

"No, thank you, Rem," Ivy said rolling her eyes.

"Better you than me," Flip called after him, waving a plastic machete, covered in fake blood.

Onyx helped D'Mario, dressed as a pizza delivery man, with more wood for the bonfire. He guessed D'Mario had come with Lettie, who was wearing a giant foam slice of pizza. Lettie, Ivy, and Jacqui in her unicorn costume lounged by a smaller fire next to the pond. Shay in a gypsy costume was inspecting Caleb's choice. He wore a white t-shirt printed with an error message, "Error 404, Costume not found."

Olivia and Harbor showed up late as a mermaid and a pirate. Harbor had the worst fake beard, an eyepatch, and a stuffed parrot that fell in the bonfire. The poor little guy was incinerated within minutes.

"Hey Onyx!" Harbor shouted at Onyx, over

everyone. "What does a pirate say on his eightieth birthday?"

"I don't know man, what?" Onyx laughed.

"Aye Matey! Ayyyem eighty!!"

Onyx put his palm to his head.

"No, Harbor."

"I'm eighty!"

"Just, no."

Caleb and Remy had installed wireless speakers into the trees earlier that week, so the music bumped through the grove and down to the water. After a few hours, Ivy seemed to relax with Everly occupied by Remy. Onyx grabbed the Oreos, chocolate, and marshmallows he brought, and made his way to Ivy for what he hoped would be the most epic s'mores.

"No way!" Ivy shouted, immediately grabbing the package.

Onyx smiled. Ivy was the best when she was happy, relaxed, and being herself. Onyx put his arm around her, but seconds later, he felt her stiffen. Everly was swaying over with Remy.

"Hey guys, you have a car she can sleep it off in, or something?"

Olivia and Ivy got up to collect Everly from Remy, but Everly pushed them away.

"I'm fine, I'm fine," Everly slurred. "Go back to stuffing your face, Ivy."

Everyone fell silent. The crickets and the pop of the fire seemed to grow louder.

"Okay, let's go," Olivia grabbed Everly's arm, but she yanked it away.

"Don't touch me," Everly snapped. "I'm having fun with Ivy and her new friends. Do you like them better than me, Ivy? Do you like dressing up like a grandma and cramming cookies down your pie hole with these losers?"

"They're my friends," Ivy stood up, crossing her arms. "They're my real friends, and I don't need fake ones."

"Oh, really?" Everly raised her eyebrows. "You look ridiculous!"

Everly teetered off on clear high heels, her giant bunny tail bouncing up and down with each haughty step.

"Where are you going?" Ivy shouted.

"To call an Uber!" Everly shouted back.

"We don't even get cell service out here," Jacqui mused.

"What's an Uber?" Flip asked.

Ivy stalked down to the edge of the water. Her heart had stopped hammering and her tears began forming behind her eyes. Ivy hated them. They were angry tears, covering up years of hurt.

"I have no chill for that girl, Ive. I sent Remy and Caleb to look for her," Onyx said, jogging down the bank. "I don't know why Remy let her drink that much."

"Right," Ivy scoffed. "It wasn't Remy who let her drink that much. She always does."

Onyx nodded. He sat down next to Ivy.

"Is she always like that?"

Ivy sniffed and nodded through tears.

"Damn, Ive," Onyx winced.

He wrapped his arms around her and let her cry, only stopping to take off his jacket and wrap it around her. Ivy burrowed into his shirt once more, wiping away her tears.

"I'm sorry about her. I'm sorry I ruined the party," Ivy whimpered.

"Don't be sorry," Onyx said. "I can't believe anyone would act like that. I can't believe anyone would treat you like that. I mean, I would never hit a girl, but- no one needs to talk to you like that. Is that why you've been so distant? This crap that chick has been putting in your head?"

Ivy shrugged.

"That's got to stop. I said I'd never try to control you or tell you what to do, but that voice in your head has to exit, like quick, okay? You are the most beautiful girl I have ever seen. Not just what's outside, but what's inside, the part you don't show to very many other people."

"I feel like that part died," Ivy admitted. "I feel like the happy part of me died with Beckett and that part got sick with my mom. I feel like I can't be happy, like I don't get to be happy. Every time Everly says something bad about me, I feel like she's right. I've felt that way for a long time, but- but since I met you, I feel more like myself, the girl that writes and plays chess and makes jewelry and has friends. It's just sometimes that voice comes back, and I try to push it away, but I end up pushing you away instead. I'm sorry. I'm just- so sorry."

"Don't be sorry, Ive," Onyx said, kissing her forehead. "I love you. I love every part of you, the Ivy that saves turtles, and likes Oreos, and writes awesome articles, and cares about people, and doubts herself sometimes, but stands up to the Stone Witch. I love the Ivy that believes in me and accepts me for who I am."

"I love you, too," Ivy said, smiling through her tears. "You are the best person I have ever met."

"Nah," Onyx shrugged. "But I try."

"Onyx!" Caleb shouted. "I found Everly and Olivia is taking her back to her hotel. She's sleeping it off. I got her email address, just in case anyone finds her bunny ears."

"Thanks, man!" Onyx shouted back. "You ready?"

"Yeah," Ivy answered. "I should probably get back home."

Onyx stood up, pulling Ivy with him. They walked back to Flip's car together to drive him home. He was passed out in the back seat with his bloody clown mask still on.

"Rabid bunnies and scary clowns," Onyx said, driving the backroads. "All in all, I'd say it was a pretty good Halloween."

CHAPTER 22

Shield Wall
Inksgate, 1132 A.D.

Morgana paced the Winter Hall, digging her nails into her palms. Harek sat on one of the tables with his head in his hands. The warriors were preparing for Jarl Gimstad's arrival. Morgana gave orders to the blacksmith to fashion the axe handles and arrows from a new species of tree Morgana had grown herself, to keep the weapons from disintegrating during a blast of earth magic.

"You are not to go. You will stay in the Winter Hall with the women and children," Harek commanded.

"No!" Morgana shouted at him. "I am going with you!"

"Do you think I cannot defeat Jarl Grimstad on my own? I have done it once, Morgana. Do you not believe in me?"

"Do you not believe in me?" she shot back. "If I do not go with you, we will surely lose more lives. You know this, Harek."

"If I am killed, who will rule Inksgate in my absence?" he asked.

"Arin and Syrine, and Alfie when he is of age."

Harek shook his head.

"Arin is coming with us and Syrine is not Viking. They will never accept her as queen."

"I am not Viking!" Morgana shouted. "How am I any different?"

"You are not going into battle and that is final!" Harek roared.

"Do not speak to me in that manner. I am queen!"

Harek dropped his head in his massive hands once more.

"It suits you," he said, bleakly.

Harek wrapped his hands around her waist and pulled her to him. He inhaled her scent, like honey and sunshine. It was the opposite of foul sweat, human waste, and metallic blood, the scents of the battlefield. The sounds were worse. Men half dead, with limbs severed crying out in anguish over the clash of swords. The battle cries masked paralyzing terror.

"You do not know what battle is. You cannot imagine," Harek said.

Morgana knew he was right. Harek shook with nightmares in his sleep, fighting off demons she would never know. Morgana took his hand in hers. A streaming, crimson ribbon of light flowed around their hands, binding them, a magical reminder of the vows they had taken.

"I cannot imagine," Morgana admitted, "but we promised. And if you take me with you, there will be no battle to speak of. You can lower your shield, Harek. You will not need it anymore."

Morgana gazed into a slab of quartz, mined for her in the cave she created by moving the cliff. In the rock, she saw Jarl Grimstad preparing his warriors for battle. He promised them their own piece of her kingdom. He promised Harek's head on a spike. He promised to enslave Morgana, to torture her until she created mountains of gold.

When she told Harek she could make gold, he declined. He said he would rather have seas of wheat fields to feed his people. He said he would rather have iron because gold was too soft to do anything useful. He had no idea why humans were so fascinated by it.

Grimstad had plans to ride into Inksgate and take everyone by surprise in the middle of the night, but when he crossed the Blue Peaks into Inksgate, Harek and his army would be waiting for them.

Harek gathered his warriors on horseback. The stallions were as fast as anyone had ever ridden. The warriors stood in rows, forming a tight circle in the middle of the field below the Blue Peaks, the border of Inksgate. Soon, they heard the thundering of hooves. The swish of air above told them that Grimstad's arrows were headed their way. They appeared to be sitting ducks.

"Shield wall!" Harek shouted to his warriors.

They immediately ducked under their shields, all save for Morgana. She pulsed a blast of light upward. Shots of the silver light lit up the sky, disintegrating the wood in the arrows. The arrowheads froze in midair and then sprinkled down like raindrops.

The archers rode down from the peaks, holding only limp bowstrings in their hands, as all the wood in their bows had been destroyed. Jarl Grimstad called the rest of his army down the peaks, surrounding Harek's warriors. A mocking laugh sounded from within the ranks, and a few moments later, a man rode forward on a pure white horse.

He was tall with a shaved head and a long beard, forked in two. His battle armor was a mountain of silver, capped off by the crested helmet he held in his hands. The armor was forged from the sets won in his conquests, worn by his enemies. Jarl Grimstad wore a sneer and a large scar over half of his face. He only had one bright blue eye.

"I see you've come to deliver my new bride along with my kingdom," Jarl Grimstad laughed, showing yellow teeth. "I shall take her and her magic along with the kingdom that is rightfully mine."

Morgana sent another pulse of light up to the sky, shattering all of the shields in Grimstad's army. The soldiers took a step back. Morgana could see in the flaming torches the fear on their faces.

"Do I frighten you?" she called to Jarl Grimstad.

"No, witch," he called back. "Do you think I wouldn't find out about your weakness? I have spies everywhere. Now, consider this a little wedding present from me to you."

From behind the ranks, a cannon blast sounded through the gorge beneath the peaks. Morgana watched as an iron spiked net flew through the sky. Harek rushed to help her, but she waved him away, growing vines up from the earth to protect herself from the net. When the net had settled on the vine canopy, a light emitted from the cracks in the vines, exploding into the air and forcing the spiked net back onto Grimstad's ranks. She had gotten a bit smarter since her last encounter with iron. Morgana raised her palms.

Grungraheten.

As she sounded into the earth, the spell reacted, growing thick, snaking vines around the rival army's feet, planting them to the earth.

"Don't move," she shouted at the opposing army. "If you value your life. Not that you could."

Harek followed Morgana as she rode her silver horse through the ranks, addressing the rival army.

"Shield maidens!" she called. "Go home. Return to your lands and children. You chose this Jarl based on his lies. Do not let his serpent's tongue lead you astray. If you leave now, you will be transported to safety. I do not wish for you to die. You will have ten seconds to make up your minds."

"Hold your lines!" Grimstad shouted at his army. "Deserters will be executed!"

The vines holding the shield maidens in place retracted, and all but three ran for the peaks, back to their villages. The three that remained howled and ran for Morgana, swords pointed. She did nothing and her own shield maidens made quick work of them in seconds.

Morgana turned to Harek. The crimson path of light traveled around her hand. A second stream of light wrapped Harek's hand in a ribbon of matching crimson.

"It's the only way," she said. "We have to do this together."

She placed her glowing palm up the peaks. As Harek did the same, echoing her motion, the peaks began to shake with a low rumble. The quake started gradually at first, then shook to a low roar, sending boulders and crags tumbling into the valley below. Jarl Grimstad glared at his army, melded to the land by the vines, snaking around their feet.

Harek's entire army retreated, galloping on horseback for Inksgate to avoid the avalanche of rocks from the peaks. Arin tossed a rope around Jarl Grimstad, capturing him, and dragging him away from the avalanche and from his usurped army, who would be buried beneath the rocks within minutes.

Harek's army rode back to camp just outside of the village, but Morgana, Harek, and Arin stopped to make sure that Grimstad was still alive and that his army was buried under the avalanche.

Grimstad's armor had kept him relatively unscathed. Arin tore off his helmet. The Jarl spat in his face.

"Kill me, you dogs. Get it over with," he growled.

Arin shook his head.

"No. We are not going to kill you," Harek said.

"But I can tell you who will," Morgana offered. "You had a Frankish servant girl once. Remember? You nearly beat her to death for overcooking one of your boars."

"She's been perfecting her roasting technique," Arin finished. "I think you'll be quite impressed with her skills."

CHAPTER 23

Moving On

Onyx couldn't believe Ivy would go back to the forest after what happened. She seemed drawn to it, but she hadn't seen the Stone Witch again.

Also on his list of astonishing stuff was the fact that Ivy was still talking to Everly after what happened on Halloween. Everly should have come dressed as the devil, he mused to himself.

"Yeah, well, she's not right," Ivy said, hiking through the forest. "When she said all that mean stuff about me. She wasn't right."

Onyx smiled. For the past few years, Everly had been pasting these invisible stickers all over Ivy. *You're not good enough. You're not pretty enough. Newspaper is stupid. Don't show any weakness or flaws. Don't try to improve yourself because people will see that you aren't already perfect.* Ivy was finally starting to pick at those stickers. She was seeing that they weren't truths, they were just judgments, and that those judgements came from someone who was wrong.

"That's what bullies do, Ive. They judge. You're either good enough or not. You either have it or you don't, and if someone else has it, all hell breaks loose. They have to knock you down so they can stay on top, and since they're on top and you're not, they can be as mean as they want. The thing is, it's not true. It's a sham, a big lie."

"Smoke and mirrors," Ivy nodded.

"Bullies judge and victims believe it, but you don't have to be a victim. You don't have to believe it. You don't believe Everly, right?" Onyx asked.

"No, and I don't believe Madison either," Ivy said.

Onyx laughed.

"I never believed Madison. She was always trying to make me someone I wasn't. Even if she thought I was one of the gifted, chosen ones, I wasn't. That's not me. I mean, I love football, don't get me wrong. Hitting stuff is the best, and scoring touchdowns- amazing, but I want to do other stuff too, and hang out with who I want."

Ivy understood. They had both been bullied by people who thought they had power over them, but it was all an illusion.

What wasn't an illusion was the macabre scene of the stone statues lining the side of the forest. The pipeline was inches away from breaking the boundary and the stone men had moved to the edge of the forest.

"They've moved, Onyx," Ivy said. "The stone men. They've moved."

"I know," Onyx shrugged. "But how? They're statues."

"I don't think they're just statues," Ivy whispered, fear lacing her low voice. "The witch said there were bodies, but they're not buried. She turned them all to stone. And the next full moon is coming. She warned us."

That night, alone in her bathroom, Ivy grabbed a pair of scissors. She surprised herself by only shedding a few tears as she cut her hair off to her shoulders. When the blonde fringe swayed past, hitting her shoulders, she wielded the scissors, cutting more until she felt free, with nothing weighing her down. Stepping out of the pool of hair around her feet, she felt as though she were stepping into her true self.

The next day, she should have been nervous about seeing Onyx, but she wasn't. She knew what he would say.

When he saw her across the courtyard, her new short fringe swaying past her jaw, he ran to her, sweeping her into his arms. He whispered into her hair.

"You have never been more beautiful."

CHAPTER 24

THE WIND AT YOUR BACK
INKSGATE, 1137 A.D.

Harek raised his hand to the level of his eyes, inspecting the fleet of longships waiting in the harbor. Morgana had grown the tallest trees anyone had ever seen. With a flick of her cloak, she cut them down into planks for Arin to use.

Once an expert shipbuilder, he lost most of the viable wood in Inksgate to the famine. The trees rotted from the inside out, but with the rot gone and the famine just a distant nightmare, Arin built the strongest fleet in existence, seemingly overnight.

In reality, it had been five years since Morgana and Harek were married. Alfie had grown and was getting stronger every day. Inksgate was a prospering hub of trade and culture. Slavery had been outlawed and for the most part, it was a time of peace. Morgana saw people of the East in the quartz stone and sent trading parties to acquire silks and weapons. Harek had stopped raiding and focused on developing new weapons based on the eastern technology the trading parties brought back. Syrine developed new medicines every day from herbs grown in the gardens surrounding the Great Hall.

Harek glanced away from the ships and turned toward Morgana.

"I can take you back," he offered.

"Where to?" she asked, reeling from the question. "We've sent warriors back to Holy Island to protect them from other raids. Father Thomas writes saying they are prosperous."

"I mean to Scotland," he answered, slowly.

Morgana snapped her head in his direction. The question fed a latent anger she thought was gone.

"To Castle Direlton?" she asked. "Why would I go back there? My parents are dead. There isn't anyone there, only roving bands of nomads and Roman deserters. We've seen it in the stones. The castle is in ruins."

"We could take it back," Harek suggested, taking her hand and soothing her ire. "It could be your home once more."

Morgana turned her head slowly, giving Harek a sideways glance.

"My home was never in the castle. My home was in the meadow, in a little hut with my mother. Until Tiernan killed her, that is."

Harek sighed and Morgana answered his silence.

"This isn't about going back for me. It's about going forward for you. Isn't it?"

Harek seemed bemused by the question. He had to admit, his queen wasn't wrong. Harek had raided all along the northern coast and into Britannia, but he longed for something different. Inksgate had become crowded and densely populated. He craved the adventure that only the open sea and untouched lands could give him. Most of all, he wanted to experience a new, wild land with the one he loved the most. Morgana seemed to sense his restlessness.

"Let's sail across the Great Sea. The boats can handle the open waters. We have a chance to do something that has never been done before."

Harek nodded, a smile forming across his lips and into the corners of his eyes. It was decided. In the next months, they set out across the open water, sailing for new land, the wind at their backs, and the open sea and sky before them.

Morgana woke up three months later, blinking into the sunlight as she had when she first arrived in Inksgate. Arin greeted her. This time, there was no sword pointing into her face.

"My queen, I am charged with bringing you ashore."

Morgana laughed and jumped up, clutching the side of the boat and taking in the riverbank.

The flat longships glided up the river with ease. They had been traveling up the river for almost a week when Harek spotted a perfect parcel of land off the water. A quiet forest bordered a sunny meadow with plentiful game. A cool, clear stream ran through the forest.

Syrine calmed Alfie, who was dying to get off the boat. When Harek and Arin pulled their boat ashore, Alfie ran off to the meadow. Harek sent a party to search the land, careful not to claim any lands already belonging to the native tribes they had seen downriver.

Harek's army shored the remaining boats. The sounds of shouting men, supplies being unloaded, and animals coming ashore filled the air, but they all faded away as soon as Harek decided on this piece of land. It was a new magic Morgana had never experienced before. The world blurred to the horizon. Sea, land, and sky melded together.

Morgana pushed past the others, stepping through the forest to an inner clearing. Before her rested a large, upright boulder. It was a flat pillar piercing the sky. Four smaller stones surrounded the pillar.

Morgana raised her hand. The runes flowed through her body, the new Viking runes, inscribing themselves onto her soul, a part of her enclosed in the magic. White hot light streamed out from her hand, hitting the stone, carving the runes into the rough, glittering surface. Small puffs of white smoke gathered around each rune, but were whisked away by the prairie winds. The markings seemed to glow.

`Merhara.`

Morgana uttered the spell, sending the light shooting for the four stones. The runes inscribed themselves onto the smaller boundary stones. When the stones had been carved, Morgana sailed them out to the corners of the land, claiming the land for the Gray King. The land vibrated with life.

After living through Jarl Grimstad's attack, she vowed that never again would anyone challenge Harek or his descendants for the Gray King's lands.

CHAPTER 25

BY THE STARS

Scott Roy shook his head. The lead engineer on the pipeline paced through the forest along the vein where the earth had been cut open. He stepped over buckled concrete. It was completely burst open, but the pipes were still intact, bent at odd angles. Scott wondered what force could buckle the steel like that.

"I don't know what happened," Scott mused, shaking his head.

"Come on, Scott. You're the best I've got," Lincoln Phillips pleaded. "Wade and Price aren't going to be happy."

"I can tell you exactly what happened, Linc," Jay Rainwater said.

"I don't want to hear it, Jay," Linc Phillips spun around. "I don't want to hear any of your ghost stories or your old wives tales or any of that. I want this pipeline done before Price's trial. If the pipeline doesn't go through, our stock will plummet. Then we'll be up a creek, so spare me the crap.

It's probably one of them hot pools or something, right Scott?"

Linc looked to Scott with a twinge of hope, but it was crushed when the engineer shook his head.

"No geothermal activity in this part of the park," Scott reasoned. "We made sure to steer clear of the pools."

"Well, tomorrow we start over," Linc groused. "Come what may, this pipeline is going through that piece of land and that's final."

Ivy paced her living room in frayed jeans, a dusty rose tank top, and a cream sweater. Her blonde hair swayed wavy, just past her jawline. Her mom motioned for her to sit down on the couch. Ivy sighed.

"You'll wear a hole in the floor," her mom smiled.

"Were you this nervous when you and dad were dating?" Ivy asked.

Camille Freya and Max Jasper had grown up together, hiking through the Oklahoma hills, then moving out to Colorado together for college. They both had always been drawn to the mountains. Ivy was born in a log cabin in the mountains, one month early. Her mom said she never wanted to wait.

"No. You kids these days, with your rock music," Camille laughed, resting after another follow up treatment. "Relax. He'll love the gift."

It was the day after Onyx's sixteenth birthday. The morning of, his mom drove him to take his driver's license test and later, they all went out to dinner to celebrate his passing score. Onyx drove the two of them to school the next morning with Ivy clutching the seat and her backpack for good measure.

"I'm not scared!" she shot back after he ran the accusation by her.

"Then hold my hand," he smiled and laughed.

Ivy shook her head violently and clutched her mint leather backpack until they were in the school parking lot.

Ivy was in doubt about a present, but she found a black Dallas Cowboys hat with a gray logo online. When it arrived, she turned it upside down and filled it with his favorite candy (peanut butter cups), his favorite black socks (no logo), and a book on chess strategies. Last and decidedly not least, she added a package of glow-in-the-dark stars for his ceiling to remind him of their first kiss by the lake.

"Crap!" Ivy squealed when the doorbell rang.

All the contents of the hat flew out onto the living room floor. Ivy extended her palm and flew the gifts back into the hat. Fixing her hair with a huffy breath, she ran to get the door. When she opened the door, her stomach did a teeny flip. Onyx was wearing a gray thermal henley and faded jeans with another black hat turned backwards. Sheesh, he's so cute with his hat turned backwards. Add another sticker to the locker, Ivy thought with a smile.

"Happy Birthday," she grinned.

"That was yesterday," he said with a small smile and a slight tilt forward. "I said hi to your dad. He's tinkering around in the garage."

Most people tinkered with cars in the garage. Max Jasper tinkered with carbon dating.

"Have a good night Mrs. Jasper," Onyx shouted into Ivy's living room.

He understood about her mom's treatments. Since they had grown closer and Onyx had seen magic in real time, Ivy spilled the beans about the gold, her fight with Ashley, and some of the things she could do with her magic. She explained that she tried not to use it, and Onyx understood. She knew it and Onyx knew, smiling over the hat full of gifts, planned out just for him. Things were serious.

"So, where are we going?" Ivy asked, climbing up into Onyx's truck.

She was excited that he could legally drive it now. She even relaxed and held his hand as they twisted through the back roads.

"You didn't look in the back of the truck, did you?" he asked, smirking.

"No!" Ivy squealed with excitement, but she couldn't look back when she tried because Onyx pinned her hand down to the seat. "Stop it! I want to look. I can't even! You are seriously so strong. You're killing me."

Onyx pulled the truck over to the side of the road, skidding to a stop on the gravel. Onyx turned to look at her.

"Ivy, you are the most beautiful girl I've ever seen. You kill me every time I look at you. I'm done. Lights out."

Onyx reached over, grabbed her seatbelt, and buckled her in. He kissed the top of her hand and kept driving. Ivy didn't know what to say. She stared at him, heart pounding.

They turned into a clearing. Onyx took out a flashlight, searching the ground for any sticks or holes. He let the tailgate down, unveiling a small mountain of pillows and blankets. Ivy's mouth dropped open. She didn't waste any time as she hopped up and snuggled in. It was getting cold at night, but Onyx plugged an electric heater into the car outlet and in no time, the truck bed was toasty warm.

"Stars for stars," he smiled, holding up the package of glow stars from his present.

"Sorry I was late," Ivy shrugged.

"You're right on time," Onyx assured her.

When he clicked off the flashlight, the sky seemed to burst with light. The clearing dulled to a pitch black and the vast expanse above them seemed to pull them in, closer to the universe and yet closer to the earth beneath them. Ivy knew that millions of light years away, and right before her eyes, there were billions of stars being born, blazing into existence and fading, dying out millimeters away as she saw them, but thousands of light years away from each other. It was life and death in motion and yet standing still, in a display barely comprehensible. It was paradoxically beautiful.

"Sailors used to navigate by the stars," Ivy murmured, too transfixed by the still ballet that was the night sky to utter her words at full volume. "Can you imagine?"

"Yes," Onyx answered. "No. Yes, though. We were created with everything we need, we just need to learn how to use it."

Ivy let his words sink in. Her magic was old, older than some of the new stars above her. She was created with it and as the next full moon drew closer, just like her mother, she knew she had to use it for good.

CHAPTER 26

WHAT HAVE YOU DONE? THE NEW WORLD, 1142 A.D.

Morgana looked at her hands, stained a deep purple from the blackberries she had gathered. The sight unnerved her that morning for some reason. The New World not only yielded crops, but held secret treasures, berries, nuts, and mushrooms for gathering. The woods were rich with wild game and each night, turkeys or venison roasted over a fire in the new Great Hall. Four years had passed since their longships traveled to the New World and each one grew sweeter, like the blackberries, ripening in the sun. Yet, in every blackberry patch, there is always one berry that sours.

Morgana sucked on her thumb, cut from the brambles in the blackberry bushes. She was usually careful, but she was nervous today. Harek and his men were going boar hunting today. Morgana hated boar. She hated the taste of it and hated boar hunting. It was dangerous. Hunting deer or turkey was different, safer. The river swam with fish and the land provided grains and vegetables. They had a pasture full of goats for milk and cheese. Still, Harek grew restless.

"Who am I? The king of the goats?" Harek asked.

He practiced his boar hunting technique day and night, as he practiced for battle. The boundary kept the neighboring tribes out. It made the forest invisible to them, so there was no need to fight over lands. Morgana had crafted the spell that way, so Harek would never need to fight for his lands again. Still, he grew more and more unsettled.

Morgana fidgeted with the satchel of berries, agitated. They were taking too long.

"Morgana!"

A voice bounced through the hollow. It had a sharp edge, slicing through her.

"Morgana, come now!"

The sound of her own name in Arin's panicked voice turned her stomach. She only froze for a moment, but it seemed like an eternity. She willed herself to move. She seemed to float out of her body.

"Now!"

Arin's voice gripped her. It pulled her out of the panic. She ran after him through the trees. He didn't have to say what happened. Morgana saw it. She felt it. She had been saving herself, storing up every magical reserve she had.

Morgana ran through the woods following Arin for what seemed like miles. She heard Harek's anguished cries before she saw him. His agony filled the forest with a pain, heavy and palpable.

"Harek!" Morgana screamed into the woods.

She pushed through the wall of his men surrounding him. Shock and terror covered their faces. In the middle of the circle of warriors, Harek lie curled up on the forest floor, clutching his side. Blood covered the ground around him. The surface of the earth was coated, the air metallic.

"I just want you with me. In the end," Harek spat out, gritting his teeth.

He reached for her. Morgana grabbed his hand and placed her other hand on the wound at his side. The boar had torn a hole in the side of his torso.

Morgana shook her head violently, panting from the run, struggling to conjure anything. Her hands glowed with the healing light, but Harek's wound remained a jagged tear in his side.

"It's not the end," Morgana pleaded.

"You fight in the face of death," Harek whispered out in a last wracked breath, amused by his queen. "You truly are Viking."

"No," Morgana sobbed. "No!"

Harek took his last breath, the life leaving his body. Morgana shook her head. She struggled to breathe. She was still trying to heal him when Arin grabbed her hand.

"He's left, my Queen. He is bound for Valhalla."

"No!" Morgana shrieked.

Her hands burnished with the latent magic. Arin stepped back. All the warriors stepped back. The markings on Morgana's face turned from a pale gray to inky black once more. The light receded from her hands, replaced by a piercing darkness. A haze formed around her, then, with one anguished scream into the heavens, Harek's body collapsed into dust. The men around him tried to run, but their skin turned a marbled purple, then gray, as they hardened into stone.

Morgana excruciated over pained breaths. She drug her hands through Harek's ashes. Her eyes went wide with horror when she surveyed the damage. The entirety of Harek's army was turned to stone. All the stone buildings collapsed into rubble.

Morgana turned sharply at the footsteps rustling behind her. Syrine and Alfie approached. Syrine dropped her basket of berries.

"Morgana, what have you done?"

The queen turned to look at Syrine. Their eyes met for a fraction of a second before Morgana herself erupted, torn apart into shards of black glass. The fragments rained down and sunk into the earth.

In her grief, the Stone Witch tethered

herself to the land, and there she remained, long after all those who loved her were gone.

CHAPTER 27

The Weakness Before Our Strength

Jacqui slapped her hand down on Ivy's pencil in Algebra, startling the row in front of her, and ignoring yet another dirty look. To be fair, Ivy had been tapping it relentlessly for the past hour and a half. That was block scheduling for you.

"You broke my favorite pencil," Ivy said with a blank stare.

She was heading into the forest with Onyx after school. In two days, the moon would be full and the stone men would come alive and claim more victims, if Morgana was to be believed. Ivy was sure the witch wasn't to be doubted.

"You're about to get on my last favorite nerve," Jacqui shot back. "What's with you?"

Their teacher shushed them with a stern look, so Ivy wrote it down in a note.

Onyx and I are going to the forest on Big Cabin reserve today to try to stop the stone Viking statues from coming alive and killing everyone in the town. We have to find a way in the next two days before the full moon.

Jacqui wrote back.

I hope you saved some drugs for the rest of us. Selfish.

"I'm serious!" Ivy hissed.

Mrs. Culpepper looked up from her desk. Seeing the paper rustling, she strode over and snatched up the note. Good thing paper is made of trees, Ivy thought, disintegrating the paper in her math teacher's hands.

"We must have termites or something," Mrs. Culpepper mused, brushing the dust off her hands into the trashcan. "How strange. Carry on girls."

When the bell rang, Ivy left Algebra headed for the newspaper room. She was working on a follow-up piece to her online privacy article. Ivy decided to leave Madison's name out of her article, but everyone knew what happened. The school was buzzing. Madison confronted Onyx about it, but he told her he didn't control Ivy or her writing and strode off.

Ivy was looking at a text from him when she bumped into a sharp shoulder blade. She reeled back from whoever it was, since they were a good four inches taller and had hit her in the eye.

"Oh, sorry," Ivy said, instinctively. She was rubbing her eye, not looking at who had bumped into her.

"Sorry for what?" a faux sweetness dripped from above. "For stealing my boyfriend? For making me look like a loser in front of the whole school?"

"Madison?" Ivy asked as her blurry vision started to clear up.

There were two of her, but she came into focus. She was wearing a pink and white striped sweater and teal slacks.

"Yes, Madison. You know, I will never understand how Onyx chose you over me. Just look at you. You look like a homeless person."

Ivy rolled her eyes. True enough, she was wearing a plain v-neck t-shirt, frayed jeans, and scuffed ankle boots from too many bonfires in the mountains outside Phoenix, but it was obvious that Madison had never seen a real homeless person.

"Why do you care what I look like?" Ivy asked. She was genuinely curious. "And why are you so mean?"

Madison didn't have an answer so she just scuffed off to her next class.

Madison's pained face nagged at Ivy all through newspaper. Sure, she was getting the side eye from other people she had hacked. There was even speculation that she rigged the online votes for the class elections, but that was a rumor that Ivy didn't start.

I am not going to feel sorry for her, Ivy

resolved. And I am not going to feel sorry for that Stone Witch either.

Ivy had begun to have strange dreams. She was following Bailey through the woods. Bailey was screaming at her. "Onyx is hurt! Ivy hurry!" Then she would wake up. She had the same dream for over a week. She wondered if there was any connection to the Stone Witch.

There are bodies, but they aren't buried.

The words and the dreams haunted her. She had to find an answer.

After school, Onyx drove by to pick her up. He brought sandwiches and cookies from the Bread Shed. Ivy ate her cookie first.

"Remy seemed out of sorts," Onyx said between bites. "His Grandpa Bud has been missing for a few hours. Rem said he takes a walk around nine when the senior ladies from Shady Pines take their walk, but he isn't back."

"He's probably drunk on toilet wine with Jacqui's Meemaw," Ivy joked. "Or bedpan wine, whatever."

"No, Rem was upset. Bud likes to be hitting the Scotch by the time Maury Povich starts to find out who's the father."

"I'm sure he'll turn up," Ivy assured him, but she was worried. She had grown fond of Bud. "Okay. Let's go."

"I don't even know what we're looking for," Onyx admitted, but Ivy did.

"We need to find the burial ground," Ivy

said. "If we find where Morgana buried the Viking warriors, they can stop the pipeline or reroute it."

"Do you think you can find the graves without us digging up an entire forest?"

It was a legitimate question. Ivy had been working on detecting minerals in the soil. Since bones are made of mostly calcium, she practiced detecting calcium spikes. Her mom was good at detecting calcium since she was calcium deficient. Ivy stopped eating. For some reason, her magic worked better when she was hungry, angry, or scared.

"Tell me all the things you like about Madison," Ivy prodded as they drove to the forest.

"No," Onyx countered, then caved. "Why?"

"I have more power when I'm hungry, mad, or scared," Ivy admitted. "And I just ate."

"Okay, I'll play," Onyx gave in. "She has good study habits."

"Good study habits?" Ivy raised her eyebrows.

"Yeah, I mean, we had all our advanced classes together and she has good study habits. Puts together a mean outline. Very organized. I know, I know, great for a lab partner, bad for a girlfriend. We were going out for all the wrong reasons."

"That doesn't make me mad," Ivy said.

"It shouldn't," Onyx said, letting go of her hand and grasping the steering wheel. "Means you're finally seeing things from my point of view.

Empathy is a beautiful thing, Ive. You said scared too, right?"

Onyx leaned over, buckled Ivy's seatbelt, and then gripped the wheel. Ivy eyes widened, lips parted, sucking in an anticipating breath. Onyx gunned the accelerator, sending them flying over the dirt backroad. Ivy's screams could have cracked the windshield.

When Onyx slowed to a stop in front of the entrance to the meadow, he felt a hard whack to the chest. It nearly took the air out of his lungs. He grabbed Ivy's balled up fist.

"That really does work," Onyx marveled.
"You think?" Ivy shouted.

Onyx hopped out of the truck before she could do any more damage. The Stone Men had moved again. The tree line was clear of the menacing warriors, but deep into the forest, a hunched shape caught their eye.

"Remy was right. That's Bud!" Ivy shouted.

They ran through the trees, feeling the temperature drop. Ivy knew they didn't have much time.

Ivy stopped, almost running into the stone shape. It was Bud alright, hunched over with a permanent frown. Ivy gripped the statue. Onyx's stunt on the road had charged her powers and the light flowed easily from her hands into the statue.

The stone began to warm as the rough texture receded. Ivy struggled to take a breath. It seemed as though her very breath, her life force was being sucked into the stone statue. Bud's face fleshed out. He began to move his limbs. The temperature cooled. Ivy tried to hurry. She could feel Morgana's spirit forming from the earth into the air.

Finally, Bud sputtered to life, coughing and spatting. He waved Ivy away, putting his hands on his knees to cough up years of unfiltered cigarette smoke. When he finally caught his breath, he set his eyes on Ivy and Onyx.

"I don't suppose either of you whippersnappers got any Scotch on ya?"

Onyx shrugged, coming up empty.

"I've seen it distilled," a cold voice sounded behind them. "Tasted the angels' share myself."

The trio spun around to see Morgana. Her marked face was cold and smooth, like marble.

"I came 'round here to help ya, lady. Didn't think you'd put a spell on me," Bud squinted at the Stone Witch.

She seemed hazy, fading in and out. The temperature cooled so that the branches began to frost over.

"Well done, young witch. Next time you will not be so lucky. I can only hold the Gray King's men back for so long. In the next cycle of the moon, havoc with be wrecked upon those who cross into this land."

"This is your spell," Ivy shouted. "Why can't you just undo it?"

"It has been carved in stone," Morgana

answered. "Now that the boundary is broken, only Harek's descendants and the ones they care about may enter unscathed. Everyone else who enters will be turned to stone or killed by Harek's men."

"But Ivy and I aren't turned to stone. We're still alive," Onyx said, pleading his case.

"No, you are not," Morgana said cryptically, fading in and out of the forest air.

"You don't look strong enough to hurt anyone," Ivy said, with a boldness surprising both Onyx and Bud.

Morgana seemed surprised herself.

"We are always weakest before our time of greatest strength, young witch. You should know as well."

Morgana's image shattered before them and fell to the ground as dust. Onyx and Ivy hauled Bud out of the forest as fast as they could. They didn't stick around to find out what Morgana's cryptic words might mean. They only had two days before the full moon. They had to stop the construction on the pipeline, the vein pressing steadily on through the Gray King's land.

CHAPTER 28

BODIES

Max and Camille Jasper worked tirelessly searching the land for anything of historical significance surrounding the Viking settlement, but there was nothing. Not a shred of pottery, not a tip of an arrow, nothing. The site had either already been excavated, or there was something darker at work. It seemed as though the settlement had vanished into thin air so long ago.

Jay Rainwater drove them into the interior forest to inspect the stone men. Camille brought an arsenal of scientific tools and tricks, but she had a feeling this might be one of those things that science just couldn't explain.

Back in Phoenix, Max and Camille had a lab at the base of the Superstition Mountains. The abandoned mines and ghost towns seemed to have claimed the mountains for themselves. There were tales of Skinwalkers prowling the canyons at night, protecting the land. Anyone who entered and met with one of the creatures would be claimed and would vanish forever.

Camille felt uneasy around the stone men. Ivy begged her parents not to go. She felt a little better knowing Onyx's dad was on board. Morgana had said something about Harek's descendants being able to travel the forest unscathed.

Ivy had so many questions. What about Morgana and Harek? Did they have children? Were there other family members with them in the party that sailed for the New World? How was Onyx connected? Did it have something to do with his family?

Ivy knew he was Native American and his family had lived on the land for ages. Onyx and his father seemed to be bound supernaturally to the land itself, but Ivy couldn't prove it.

"I'll be fine, Ivy pie," her mother said over her morning coffee. "Besides, I'm your mother, I'm supposed to be worrying about you, not the other way around."

Ivy still worried. Camille was just now strong enough to travel. Max and Jay had traveled into the forest to collect samples from the stone men, but the results were always inconclusive. They needed Camille and they knew it, so that morning, they set out on four wheelers for the forest.

Camille didn't need a map to find the first stone statue. She could sense the stone. It had a unique element signature she'd never felt. The farther they drove into the forest, the more she could sense the grief, regret, and loss.

When she was very young, Liz Freya told all five of her girls, Camille, Patricia, Cynthia, Louisa, and Megan, "a witch will always turn pain into power."

This was powerful magic born from intense pain.

When the first stone statue came into view, a wave of sick dread flowed into her core. She felt the twisted stomach, not of physical pain, but emotional.

"We need to take a sample and leave, quickly," Camille commanded, feeling the temperature cool. It was a sign of an entity present, someone intelligent, old, and powerful.

Max and Jay nodded. Max jumped off the four wheeler with his kit in one hand. He had taken thousands of samples, but this one was different. He knew by the tone of his wife's voice, that this was urgent. He scraped a sample of stone off the statue, not needing a chisel. The stone was soft and porous, like pumice, but grainy like sandstone. Max Jasper's geology career spanned two decades and five continents, but he had never seen stone like this. He couldn't help but stop and marvel at its unique properties.

"Max! Hurry!" Camille shouted.

Max stuffed the sample into an envelope, snapped a few pictures, and ran back to the four wheeler. Camille was clutching her stomach. She was squinting, trying to hold back tears. The four wheelers roared to life. Camille glanced back into the forest. She could hear a voice, but couldn't make out the words.

Camille wondered if Ivy had seen the Stone Witch. Ivy warned her to hurry in the forest. Tomorrow, the moon would be full and the Stone Witch told them her warriors would come alive if the boundary was still crossed.

The four wheelers roared back to the lab at the ranger headquarters. Camille jumped off and ran inside. Max followed with the sample. They both went to work with Jay looking over their shoulders and asking questions.

"How do you know how old the sample is?" he asked.

Max answered while he worked.

"It all has to do with carbon. There's a small amount of Carbon-14 in every living organism. Carbon-14 is made when plants go through photosynthesis, breaking down sunlight into food. If an animal eats plants or eats an animal that had eaten plants, there will be Carbon 14 in their body. All we have to do is measure the amount of Carbon-14. It has a certain half life, and we can estimate with a good amount of certainty how much time has passed since the organism was alive, based on the half life of the Carbon-14."

"And by organisms, you mean the statues?" Jay asked, clarifying, trying to wrap his head around the notion.

"If my theory is correct, then yes," Camille interjected. "That the statues aren't statues."

Camille paused. Her eyes widened.

"What is it?" Max asked. "How many half lives?"

Camille paused, shaking her head. Jay looked on, trying to make sense of the numbers on the screen, but they were like a foreign language. They might as well be runes.

"None," Camille finally answered. "No half lives. This piece of stone has as much Carbon-14 as you or me."

"My god, are you sure?," Max asked.

"So, they're dead?" Jay still wasn't following.

"Or undead," Camille said, bleakly.

Max nodded.

"What does that mean?" Jay asked, still in disbelief.

"They're still alive," Camille answered. "These stone... men. They're all still alive."

CHAPTER 29

Footsteps Behind You

The night of the full moon fell on a Friday, so that meant Friday night lights for Onyx and the rest of the Big Cabin Bulldogs. Carter Willis, their senior quarterback had dislocated his throwing shoulder against the Coweta Tigers last week. Ivy wished she could help, but since it was a joint and not a bone, there was nothing she could do.

Big Cabin didn't have a backup quarterback on the varsity team, so Trystan was called up from the freshman team. Onyx said he was surprised at how efficiently Trystan was able to get the ball to him. He would be able to score now more than ever since Trystan was faster, smarter, and more accurate with his throws than Carter ever was.

The Big Cabin Athletic Park complex was set in the middle of a cornfield. Concession stands bordered a small splash pad and playground for younger siblings. The older grade school kids threw their own footballs around on the practice field.

The sun was barely starting to set when the Bulldogs took the field against the Pawhuska Huskies. Ivy shifted behind her camera on the sidelines. The Pawhuska team was huge and it was Trystan's first varsity game. Ivy hoped he wouldn't be too nervous. She was nervous enough for the entire stadium.

Ivy was inching along, trying to get a good shot of Trystan for the paper, when she bumped into someone on the sidelines. The instinctive reflex shot out before she realized who it was.

"I'm sorry!"

Ivy turned and saw that she had bumped into none other than Madison again, talking to the band director. Madison's look of fury softened at Ivy's apology. The wheels in Ivy's head spun. Let's try a little experiment, she thought.

"I'm sorry, Madison," Ivy repeated. "I really didn't mean to get in your way. I was just trying to take a picture of Trystan for the paper."

"It's okay," Madison sighed in a huffy breath. "I was just about to move on. I don't know why I was standing there anyway."

Madison began to tear up. She looked up into the lights and started to fan her eyes so she wouldn't ruin her mascara.

"We're not talking about me bumping into you anymore, are we?"

"No," Madison cried, tilting her head back a little too dramatically for Ivy's taste, but she was compelled.

"What's wrong?" Ivy asked, now genuinely curious.

"Trystan asked me out," Madison sniffed.

Well, that's unexpected, Ivy thought to herself.

"You don't like him? He seems nice- and- um- your type."

Madison shook her head, sending the massive, shiny bow on top swaying.

"I do! He's amazing. He dresses so perfect and he always listens to my ideas and he's so good looking, it's just- he's a freshman. I can't go out with a freshman. What will people say? I don't know why I'm telling you all this. I hate you," Madison sniffed. "You stole my boyfriend."

I didn't steal him, Ivy thought, but opted to take another route.

"Okay, fair enough, and I am actually sorry about that, but how long have you liked Trystan?"

Madison didn't say anything, so Ivy continued.

"As long as I've liked Onyx?"

Madison laughed.

"Trystan was looking at you during freshman orientation and I was so jealous. I thought, she's going to start dating Trystan and I'm going to be stuck with Onyx, that chess-playing loser. Isn't that messed up?"

"Kinda," Ivy laughed.

"I gotta go cheer," Madison said, walking

off, but turning back after a few steps. "You think it's okay to date a freshman?"

"Onyx does," Ivy answered. "Who cares what people think? Besides, he may be a freshman, but he is the quarterback."

"Point taken," Madison shrugged, then stopped. "He loves you, Onyx does. Like, one girl to another, that boy is in love with you."

"Thanks," Ivy said, looking down. "I love him, too."

She didn't know what else to say. The sun was starting to dip below the horizon, illuminating the tassels in the corn field. The game had just chipped into the first quarter and Onyx had already scored. Ivy was so lost in thought about the stone men that she missed it.

Ivy gave her camera to Jacqui and went to get some water at the concession stand. The game had started so the line was fairly empty. Ivy stood behind a family of five, watching the kids weave in and out of their parents' legs. Ivy laughed watching them, not hearing the footsteps behind her. She felt a tap on her shoulder.

"Whoa," Ivy gasped, spinning around. "You scared me."

A tall, muscular guy with dark blonde hair and dewy, just-showered skin shifted in jogger-style track pants and sneakers, directly behind her. His hair curled around his ears and flopped over, curling over his eyebrow in a shaggy, grown-out mohawk. He raked his hand through his hair, pushing it out of his eyes.

"I'm sorry," he said. "I don't want to bother you. You just look like someone I knew once."

"Do you go to Pawhuska?" Ivy asked.

"Yeah, this is my first year there. I'm a sophomore."

Ivy nodded. She glanced at the steel symbol dangling around his neck. A circle with a slash through the center. It was the Alchemist's symbol, the sign for salt. The guy cleared his throat.

"Do you know Ashley Nirran?"

"Yeah, she's my cousin," Ivy answered him with a mixture of shock and recognition. The guy didn't have to tell her who he was. Ivy knew it was Blaze, the Alchemist's son Ashley pulled out of the fire. "Do you want me to tell her you said hi?"

"No," he answered quickly. "It's okay. I miss her a lot, but it's better if she doesn't know where I am. It's complicated. Is she okay?"

Ivy nodded again, chewing on her lip. He was right. The less either of them knew, the better. Thank goodness Aunt Megan told them all that Ashley could only see the past, not the present or the future.

"Okay, well, thanks." The guy paused before striding off. He took one finger and brushed it across the lip she had been chewing. "Your cousin does that. I will never get over her. Not in a thousand years."

What a weird night, Ivy thought as she

watched him walk away, and it's probably about to get even more strange.

The sun dipped below the fringed horizon of the cornfield during halftime. Ivy paced the sidelines snapping more pictures of the horizon than the game. The shadows in the cornfield unnerved her. Her dead cell phone sat nagging at her in her back pocket. It was a good thing it was dead or else Ivy might have been tempted to call Ashley and tell her that boyfriend number two was still an Alchemist and still looking for her.

The game rolled on with Big Cabin up by two touchdowns. The stadium lights prevented her from seeing anything beyond the field. Tension gnawed at her stomach. Morgana's voice echoed in her head.

The ball was on the ten with eighteen seconds to go. Ivy watched the end zone to snap the perfect picture for the paper. She was watching Trystan through her lens, making sure to catch whatever his next move might be, when she saw it.

A shadow moved steadily through the corn tassels, only visible in the camera lens. Ivy thought she might be seeing glare from the lights. She lifted the lens, looking at the field with naked eyes.

It's only the shadow from the irrigation system, Ivy thought to herself. In her panic, she missed Trystan's perfect pass to Flip in the end zone. Ivy cursed to herself and hoped Jacqui had gotten the picture. When she looked back to the cornfield, the shadow was gone.

The win over Pawhuska was a big one, so the students rushed the field. It was the perfect disguise for Ivy to run out to Onyx.

"Ive!" Onyx took his helmet off to give her a big smile and a sweaty hug.

Had he forgotten about the stone men? Ivy was happy about his win, but she had to talk to him.

"We have to get home. It's the full moon and the pipeline is still moving through the forest. The stone men are going to be released. My mom called earlier and said to come home after the game, just be safe. She said they tried to carbon date them and they have just as much carbon as you or me, just as much as any living person."

"Ivy," Onyx looked at her with sincere, gray eyes. "They're statues in the forest. You said it yourself, turning Bud really took it out of her. The Stone Witch is getting weaker by the minute. Do you think that the stone men could really come alive and cross the boundary?"

"Not alive but, undead."

"Like a zombie?" Onyx asked, tilting his head.

"Exactly."

"I don't think so," Onyx said, dragging a hand through sweat-soaked hair, "but everyone is going to party on main street, so they'll all be in one place. If anything happens, we can help get everyone to safety."

Onyx was making sense. If they just hid out and did nothing, the stone men could steamroll the whole town, but if they stayed on their toes, they might prevent something terrible from happening.

Ivy explained the whole plan to her mom using Onyx's phone and charging hers in the truck. Camille agreed, but she was too weak from the forest to go. Camille couldn't believe Ivy had seen the Stone Witch and lived to tell about it, but she had her own ideas about Jay and Onyx Rainwater. She told Ivy that as long as she was with Onyx, she would be safe. The Stone Witch had left her alive for a reason.

They drove to Main Street after Onyx showered. His hair was still wet on the way into town. His t-shirt clung to his ribcage, expanding and contracting. Ivy could tell he was nervous.

"I almost forgot about the full moon," Onyx admitted. "Football makes me forget."

Ivy nodded. She knew the feeling. When she was taking pictures or designing a new piece of jewelry, she forgot for a split second everything that was wrong in the world. When she was with Onyx, she didn't forget, but somehow, she had a sense that everything was going to be alright.

Main Street was strung with lights and everyone was celebrating the big win. Onyx and Ivy paced the sidewalk. They passed the old school, now converted into an administration building, the hardware store, and Meatballs, which sat on the end of main street, surrounded by a few small craftsman style houses. Onyx turned sharply. Ivy followed.

Onyx quickened his pace through a back alley, leading to a field behind the houses. He turned back to Ivy, motioning for her to follow. Her parents always gave her pepper spray for human attackers, but she had a feeling this was going to be different. Onyx turned back to the field when he heard the footsteps behind him.

Ivy froze when she saw him. The stone man was slow, dragging stone feet through the edge of the field. He moved with a disjointed motion, as if he were once alive, but had forgotten how to move like humans do. They watched him in silence. He wasn't looking at them until Onyx stepped forward onto a piece of sheet metal.

When the metal scraped against the concrete, the stone man's head turned slowly, his blank gray eyes fixing on both of them. He stopped his movement in the field and turned toward them. The slow, jerking footsteps drug the stone warrior closer to them.

"Don't panic," Ivy whispered.

"We can't go back to Main Street. We'll lead him to everyone in the town," Onyx whispered back with a shaking voice. "What are we going to do?"

Ivy sucked in a breath. She had no idea if this would work or not, but she had to try.

"If Morgana can make a boundary, then so can I," she turned to Onyx. "You're going to have to duck."

Ivy thought back to Ashley banishing the shadow phantom. She must have used a spell, but which one? Her mom said that all their spells came from the time of the Druids. It was old and powerful magic and it only came to them in times of need. Ivy cleared her mind and called on her ancestors. Surely she was more in need now than ever.

Ivy couldn't explain it. It was like she was seeing Morgana, beautiful, happy, and young, in real time, in the present, crafting her spell to make the boundary. Sensing no signs of life inside the building, Ivy uttered Morgana's own spell into an abandoned stone building.

Merhara.

Onyx ducked down just as all of the stones exploded out from the base of the building. The stone pieces sailed to the edges of the town, encompassing Big Cabin, surrounding it with Ivy's spell, with protection from the earth.

Onyx looked up just in time to see the stone man crumble into dust.

CHAPTER 30

News To Me

Camille rushed to Ivy the second she hit the door. She was home now, but the explosion from the spell caused mass chaos on Main Street.

Most people thought a bomb had gone off. The blast from the stone building had made a huge explosion that left everyone on Main Street running, screaming, and searching for safety. People were ducking into the shops and restaurants, under tables, behind doors, crowding in kitchens and bathrooms, and looking for their loved ones.

Onyx and Ivy ran for Meatballs where Jay, Tiffany, and Bailey Rainwater were waiting for them to eat dinner. They found Jay standing in front of a booth where Tiffany and Bailey were crouching under a table. Bailey was clutching a butter knife.

It took them over an hour to drive back to Ivy's house in the confusion and traffic. They didn't get to eat since the restaurant closed immediately after the explosion, so everyone was relieved that

Camille had made an enormous vat of pork chili verde. It was Max's favorite dish from the desert, the house specialty from their favorite restaurant at the base of the Superstition Mountains.

Camille dished up the tender, stewed pork with some of the garlic and chiles from the broth. She piled each plate with refried beans, and fresh homemade tortillas, then topped everyone's pork with *queso fresco*, cilantro, *crema*, and a fried egg.

For the first twenty minutes after they sat down to eat at the large picnic table outside their small shotgun house, everyone was pretty quiet, consumed with eating, but Jay interjected.

"I don't know how much I'm supposed to say," Jay said strategically when Bailey got up to go to the bathroom, "but the blast in the building, did that have anything to do with the stone men?"

Camille glanced at Ivy, who for the first time in her whole life, heard her mother's voice inside her head.

They know about the stone men because of the carbon dating, but don't tell them about our powers.

"I don't know," Camille shrugged. "Anything is possible."

Ivy grabbed Onyx's hand underneath the table.

"What a polite young lady," Camille complimented Bailey when she put her napkin in her lap and cut her meat into perfect tiny princess bites.

Camille was trying to change the subject, but she really did think Onyx's little sister was adorable.

"Thank you," Bailey responded before Tiffany could. "I wanna be like Ivy. She uses her good manners, and is pretty, and has cool clothes, and has big boobs!"

"Bailey!" Tiffany and Jay both hissed in unison.

"Oh my god, Bay," Onyx shook his head.

Ivy turned a bright shade of red, completely mortified, but her parents both just laughed.

Onyx ate three platefuls before his exhaustion kicked in. Jay and Tiffany had to drag Bailey out to the car. She didn't want to leave, but within seconds of being on the road, she was sound asleep.

After they left, Ivy helped her mom with the dishes.

"I heard you," Ivy said, still surprised.

"I know," her mom said, smiling and taking her hand. "Was it you, that made the blast?"

Ivy nodded.

"You made a boundary?" Camille smiled. "The spell came to you or did you reach for it?"

"I don't know," Ivy shrugged. "It was weird, it was like I was standing with Morgana while she made her own boundary. I was watching her, so I knew how to do it. I sent the stones around Big Cabin and Heavener, so everyone involved with the pipeline will be safe."

"You amaze me every day, Ivy Jade," Camille said, "but I want you to be careful."

"Camille!" Max shouted into the kitchen. "Come look at this!"

Camille rushed into the living room to find Max standing in front of the evening news. Ambulances and police cars surrounded a hotel Ivy recognized as the Sunset Inn just outside of town. The reporter's voice seemed to be coming from the end of a long tunnel. She sounded distant and removed.

"-strange and unusual case. The two victims were workers on the pipeline. Phillips Oil has yet to comment-"

Ivy felt dizzy and light headed.

"-the workers were staying at a hotel outside of town. The two men were contractors for the piping supply company, Barlow Pipe and Supply, a subsidiary of Barlow Industries-"

Oh no, Ivy thought. I just put a protective boundary around the town, anyone connected to the pipeline outside of the town isn't safe.

"-one of the most gruesome murder scenes we've come across. The victims seemed to have been killed with a large axe of some sort-"

Like a Viking battle axe, Ivy thought, grimly. She knew it was one of the stone men who killed the contractors.

Camille's phone rang the instant the news went to a commercial. She spoke softy into the phone. When she ended the call, her brows knit together in worry.

"What?" Ivy asked.

"They're on their way," Camille answered. "Patricia, Megan, and Ashley are on their way."

CHAPTER 31

Below The Surface

The following Monday at school, Ivy slumped in her chair. She spent all weekend stewing over what had happened. Everyone involved in the pipeline must have stayed in town, under the protection of the barrier, because there were no more deaths, but that wouldn't last long.

Ivy tapped her pencil against her notebook, earning her a stern look from Jacqui. She decided to quit with the tapping.

The last person Ivy wanted to see was Ashley. Ivy had tried her best on the spell, but two people were dead as a result of the stone men.

The entire school was on lock down because of the murders, but construction on the pipeline was still moving. Linc Phillips insisted on it. He was on the news last night saying that the pipeline construction would continue, no matter what.

Ivy tried to focus on her classes, taking scattered notes here and there, but when the bell rang, she flew out of class, like she was being chased. She ran into Onyx in the hallway.

"Hey," he wrapped his hands around her shoulders, "I have practice after school, but I can skip it if you want me to drive you home."

"I can't," Ivy shook her head. "My dad is picking me up. My aunts and my cousin are in town."

"Which one? Harbor's girlfriend, the one you don't like, or the one you've never seen?"

"Ashley," Ivy rolled her eyes. "Ashley is the one I don't like. Olivia is Harbor's girlfriend, Ariel is the one I've never seen. She lives on the Georgia coast, but Ashley will for sure be here in about an hour."

"Okay, well, no catfights. Or witch fights, or whatever you guys do."

Ivy laughed.

The car ride was smooth through the hills. Her dad drove them to a large, secluded lodge up in the woods where they would meet the rest of their family. The lodge was a stunning log home nestled into a valley about a half hour west of Big Cabin. It bordered a lake and a stone cliff, with a large fire pit beside the lake. It was stunning. Ivy wondered if they had rented it. Her mother was already there. Ivy wondered if she would come out to meet them.

Patricia was the one who slid out the door to meet them. She was trailed by her fiery red hair, long and straight down her back. She donned a cashmere wrap over a camel chiffon blouse and black leather leggings. Olivia and her mom, Helen followed in a gray maxi dress and a tailored navy suit, respectively. Ashley trailed in yoga pants and a light blush wrap, making her auburn hair light up.

"It's amazing," Max admired. "I'm just glad we could help."

"We could help with what?" Ivy asked. Not getting an answer right away, she turned to Patricia and Helen. "We're so glad we could help with what?"

"With the purchase of the lodge, Ivy," Patricia said, calmly as if she were placating a tiger. "We needed a home base, a place where we could all stay together. Somewhere we could travel to easily. This was perfect."

"So, you made her conjure more gold?" Ivy screeched. "I hate you. I freaking hate you! Why would you let her do that? She almost died!"

She couldn't believe they would do this again. They would deplete every mineral in her mother's body just to buy some stupid lodge. Ivy was livid. Her skin turned a marbled purple. A small tremor shook the ground.

"Ivy," Max took a stab at calming her down, but it wasn't working.

"Where's my mom? Where is she?"

Ivy pushed past Ashley, running up to the front door of the lodge. She yanked the door open scanning for her mother.

"She's upstairs!" Ashley called.

Ivy ran up the stairs to the second floor balcony. She swung all the doors open until she found a large bedroom with a pale, gray skinned woman lying in bed. Her cheeks were hollowed and her hair hung stringy and lifeless, but the woman in the bed wasn't her mother.

"Aunt Cynthia?" Ivy asked, breathless from both running and shock.

Her Aunt Cynthia, Camille's oldest sister, turned her head to Ivy.

"You know," she croaked, "in some places, water is more valuable than gold."

Ivy didn't know what to say. Her mother and her Aunt Megan were preparing a healing solution. Megan's whole body glowed opalescent while she poured various vials and glasses into a large, flat disc. The shallow bowl shape seemed to float in midair. When Megan was satisfied with her work, she placed her hands around the disc and flowed the solution into a glass bottle. The solution concentrated in on itself and shone a silvery blue.

"Get the others," Megan said. "It will take all of us."

As Camille rushed outside to gather their family, Ivy asked the question burning the tip of her tongue.

"How did you do this, Aunt Megan?"

Megan Nirran smiled.

"It's complicated really, but I was blessed

with my new powers when one of the other Healers died. Our magic doesn't die with us when we do. Sometimes it gets transferred to our children, sometimes it gets absorbed back into the elements, and sometimes it just roams until it finds a host. When the last Healer in North America died, the magic passed to me."

"The Seer is surfacing in tomorrow to anoint her," Cynthia interrupted.

Megan shushed her, soothingly. She didn't want Cynthia to exert any more energy than was necessary.

"I'm sorry, the Seer? Olivia mentioned something about her, but who is she?"

Megan began before Cynthia could.

"I've done a lot of reading in the past few months," Megan explained. "The Seer is the ruler of the fates. There is Past, Present, and she is Future. She's always a water witch and can surface through even a drop of water."

"I'm sorry, what's surfacing?" Ivy asked.

"Surfacing means to travel through your element," Megan clarified. "Water witches can travel through water, fire witches can travel through fire, earth witches can travel through the earth or the stones, and air witches can fly. The lodge was perfect since anyone who needs healing can travel through their element to get to me."

"I've never seen anyone fly," Ivy slipped the suspicious comment into the conversation, but Aunt Megan had an answer.

"Of course not. They're wrapped in air when they do it," Megan said.

"That's news to me."

Ivy was left reeling. She thought she knew so much. She would have to make more time to study some of the texts in Aunt Cynthia's attic.

"Are you ready?" Patricia asked, bursting through the double doors to the large bedroom, bringing the rest of the coven with her.

"As I'll ever be," Cynthia answered. "I wish Louisa and Ariel were here."

Patricia nodded. Cynthia took the drink from Megan. Ivy was entranced by the shine. It seemed as though Ashley and Olivia were, too.

The family joined hands in a circle around Cynthia. As the potion flowed into her mouth and then through her body, her skin turned from a deathly gray to a glowing peach, her hair grew back in, glossy and bouncy, and her face plumped. She looked even younger and more beautiful than before, but she still had her flowing, silver hair.

"I would have done it for your mother if I could have, Ivy," Megan looked at her squarely. "I didn't have my powers back then. The old Healer was still alive, but I want you to know."

Ivy nodded.

"She knows," Camille assured. "We all know."

Sensing the tension, Olivia took her hand.

"Come on, let's go outside and sit by the lake."

"Okay," Ivy agreed.

The air off the water was cool, so Olivia turned on the fire pit. Patricia and Ashley seemed to sense their element within minutes.

"Mind if we join you?" Patricia asked, seeming to appear out of thin air.

Ivy shrugged.

"Did you guys surface in through the fire pit?" Olivia asked.

"Yeah," Ashley answered. "It was a tight squeeze, but we managed. What about you? Did you come through the lake?"

"No," Olivia replied. "Grandma Cynthia's water magic skipped a generation. Mom doesn't have any magic so we drove. It's not that far."

Patricia looked down. Ashley bit her lower lip. Ivy decided to break the tension.

"How do you do it? Surfacing?" Ivy asked.

"It's just like walking," Patricia answered. "You just walk through your element, but you have to save someone's life before you can. You have to prove you'll use your magic for good."

Ivy thought back to Ashley pulling Dom and Blaze out of the fire. She wondered who Patricia had saved.

"Who's life did you save, Aunt Patricia?"

"Just someone I used to know," she answered, poignancy tainting her voice.

Ivy sighed and leaned back in her chair. She allowed herself to be entranced by the flames. If you had to use your magic for good, if you had to save someone's life to be able to surface, then Ivy would never be able to. She had already allowed two people to be killed with her spell's failure.

She knew she couldn't fail again. The stone men were very real and so was the pipeline. Ivy just had to figure out how to stop it.

CHAPTER 32

It Takes Two

The next day, Big Cabin let out for Thanksgiving break. Onyx and the whole team were excited about the playoffs, but the excitement was dampened by the murders. Onyx pulled Ivy into an empty classroom after school. He was planning on talking to her about doing some research over the break, but she looked so cute in a messy bun and his slouchy hoodie, chewing on one string, that he couldn't help himself.

"Can I kiss you?"

"I wish you'd stop asking," Ivy pouted, then smiled. She jumped into his arms, pressing her lips to his. "You're never getting this hoodie back."

"I don't want it back. It looks better on you," he murmured, leaning in to kiss her, wrapping a hand around the nape of her neck.

After ten way-too-fast minutes, Ivy pulled away.

"I have to go," she whined. "You're gonna make me late for the bus."

"Hey, it takes two, Ive," Onyx winked.

"Yeah, yeah," she rolled her eyes.

Ivy rode with her mother to the lodge with the memory still fresh in her mind. Did Onyx have to have football practice every dang day, she groused to herself. It didn't matter. The Seer was surfacing today to anoint her Aunt Megan as a new Healer. Ivy glanced to the side at her mom, driving her car to the lodge. Her mom was finally strong enough to drive and the simple act of being alone in a car with her mother brought the sting of tears to Ivy's grassy green eyes.

When they arrived, the family was standing around the lake. Cynthia Stiles, her daughter, Helen Stiles-Tamesis, and Helen's daughter, Olivia wore dark navy cloaks, fastened with the water element symbol, an inverted triangle. Camille nodded to her sisters, Cynthia and Patricia, as she wrapped a dark charcoal cloak around Ivy's shoulders. It was the girls' first ceremony and the Seer expected traditional dress. Megan handed her sister Camille two earth broaches, an inverted triangle, slashed through with a line, matching her own, fastening a deep forest green cloak. Megan's daughter Ashley, wore a bright red cloak, fastened with a triangle, the symbol for fire. Ashley's broach matched her Aunt Patricia's, fastening a deep crimson cloak.

Patricia glanced at the fire pit. Seconds later, it erupted into flames. Cynthia flicked a light spray of water into the flames, while Megan gathered a handful of grass, sprinkling it on the fire. Camille added a small handful of sand.

"I wish she were here too," Camille said, smiling forlornly to Cynthia, who now fully healed, placed a feather in the flames.

"For Louisa," she whispered.

After the feather was placed, the surface of the lake began to shimmer, metallic like an oil slick, with many colors. The water solidified into a white cloak. The cloak was empty, until a human shape formed in the water, filling the empty cloak. Gray hair spilled from the hood and a face materialized, followed by a body. The old woman sank a bit in the water, finding her footing on the lakebed, then crossed the shoreline. She dried as soon as she crossed onto the shore.

"Cynthia," the Seer nodded to her aunt. "It's so good to see you. I do miss your mother. Liz Freya was an incredible woman."

Cynthia tipped a slight nod. Patricia sucked in a shaking breath. Camille and Megan clasped hands. It was clear that all the Freya girls missed their mother. She passed away shortly after her husband was lost to pancreatic cancer. Liz and Karl Freya were one of life's great love stories and it was hard on the girls to lose both of their parents so close together.

The Seer glanced around the circle.

"I see you are missing your air witches," the Seer sent a loaded glance to Cynthia, then continued, "but I see you have two fire witches in your coven. How nice for you. They're very rare. Very unusual."

"Yes, we are fortunate," Cynthia returned. "And Louisa does send her regrets."

The ceremony continued with the Seer anointing Megan with four oils, one for each element, and sprinkling her with salt. The ceremony didn't really give her any additional powers, she already had them, but it did connect her to the Light. If anyone needed to find her, they would be able to come to her to be healed.

"We don't perform miracles," the Seer warned. "No one can do that, but we do use our powers for good and we help when we are needed."

When the ceremony was over, the Seer sunk back into the lake. The water glowed where she went under. Ivy watched as her light receded into darkness.

When their robes were safely back in the coven chest, everyone sat down at the long table in the lodge's great room. Helen and Megan had been cooking again. The dining room table was soon filled with platters of pasta, salads, and loaves of garlic bread. Ivy made sure to sit between her mother and Olivia. She didn't want to deal with Ashley after the Seer had basically told her she was some special witch princess.

"How's it going," Olivia asked during dinner. "You know, with your problem in the forest?"

Olivia twirled a forkful of linguine on her

spoon and popped it into her mouth. She followed it with a forkful of salad before her eyes went wide.

-I can hear you, she thought.

-Yeah, I know, ain't it great? Two people are dead because of me and the pipeline is still going through the forest.

-It's not your fault. You're doing what you can. I know you and Aunt Camille will figure out a way to stop the pipeline.

Ivy grabbed Olivia's hand under the table. A warmth radiated through their hands that could only be described as family. They might have stayed that way all night if Helen hadn't brought out a chocolate mousse.

As they were leaving, Ashley jogged out the front door and down the stone steps to the circle drive in front of the lodge. Ivy was just about to get in the car.

"Hey," Ashley shouted. "Good job on the boundary. My mom told me about it. I don't know how you reached for that spell. Mine just kind of came to me."

"Right," Ivy nodded and turned to get in the car.

"Did you think that it was Aunt Camille?" Ashley asked after her. "Did you think that Aunt Camille was the one who conjured more gold to pay for the lodge? Because Cynthia and Patricia totally didn't want her to."

"Would you just stop talking to me?" Ivy snapped.

"What did I do?" Ashley asked.

Ivy paused when she saw a flash of true pain cross her cousin's porcelain face.

"Nothing," Ivy softened her tone, but not her heart. "Just leave me alone."

"Look, I'm trying but-"

"It's all about you," Ivy cried, the hurt and fatigue betraying the disguise of anger she had so carefully crafted. "You're the special fire witch. You got your spell right on the first try. No one died because of you. You'll never understand."

Ivy shut the door, leaving her cousin silent on the steps. Camille, sensing her sadness just drove. She knew what it was like to feel that you'd never measure up to the fire witch in the family.

The next day, after a fitful sleep, Onyx and Ivy headed to the Big Cabin Public Library with more sandwiches from Bud's Bread Shed. They were free this time. Bud insisted.

"Okay," Onyx sighed, pacing down the section on parapsychology, "we got witches, goblins, werewolves, and.... here it is. Zombies."

They settled down at a table under the original gilded, art deco ceiling. It was a beautiful library and Ivy found herself wishing they were there under happier circumstances.

"I wish I brought you here sooner," Onyx admitted. "You know, when we weren't dealing with the end of the world. I normally love coming here to play chess. I like military history, too."

"I would be all about the science fiction," Ivy said.

She was too excited that Onyx was on the same wavelength. She forgot all about hiding her nerdy side. Then again, she didn't really have to with him.

"I love Star Wars. I'd totally be Vader."

"Yeah, you'd totally be Vader," Ivy said, agreeing.

Onyx and Ivy paged through the books until Ivy came to an interesting page.

"Okay, listen to this. In Haitian lore, a zombie is an undead entity made from the animated human remains of a person. The zombie is created by a sorceress and the ruler of the tribe, together."

"It takes two," Onyx said.

"Yep, it takes two," Ivy echoed. "There's more. The zombies created by the sorceress will only be reverted back to their original state, upon the death of the sorceress."

Ivy stopped reading. The last part confused her. She didn't know how they could kill Morgana if she was already dead. She had been alive since the time of the Vikings, surely she was dead. Or was she? The thought made Ivy's head hurt.

"We just have to find out how to kill Morgana," Onyx said.

Ivy could hear the twinge of sadness in Onyx's voice. She felt it too. Kill Morgana. Ivy felt sorry for her. She had seen her marked face, felt her pain, but still, it seemed like the only way. The only way to save the town was to get rid of the stone men, and that meant getting rid of Morgana herself.

CHAPTER 33

THE UNDEAD

Onyx closed the book. Ivy started talking as soon as the cover slammed shut.

"We have to go back into the forest tonight," she insisted. "We have to figure out how to kill Morgana."

"She's got to be dead. I mean, she's been alive for a long time," Onyx said, honestly confused. "Besides, I don't want you going into the forest. You could be hurt, or even killed."

"Not if you go with me," Ivy pressed. "Remember, she said Harek's descendants could come and go on the land. I'm sure that's why she was looking at your blood when she first saw you, when you fell in the forest."

"You think?" Onyx asked.

"Yeah, I mean, think about it. The stone men are all men, all warriors. No women or children, but Morgana and Harek must have had children. They must have assimilated into the native tribes on the land when Morgana created the stone men."

Onyx didn't know. It was an interesting theory and it was worth going back into the forest to see if they could find Morgana to ask her. If she could tell them anything, maybe they could get the pipeline stopped.

So, the night before Thanksgiving, Ivy slipped out of her bedroom window to meet Onyx. He parked far away so Max Jasper wouldn't hear him approaching. Camille was driving around, looking for the stone men. She had to be careful. One blast of magic to one of the stone men could deplete her reserves permanently. It could render her unmagical or even worse, it could kill her, but she didn't want Ivy to go.

In the truck, Ivy pulled her knees to her chest. Onyx could tell she was nervous and feeling guilty for going out when her mom told her not to, but she insisted on pressing into the park and deeper into the forest. Onyx knew she couldn't sit by and do nothing. As they neared the forest, they saw a slim figure, silhouetted against the moonlight.

Onyx squinted. The figure was stone still in the waning moon, but it didn't look like one of the tall, broad warriors. Besides, Onyx concluded, the stone warriors wouldn't be on the land, they would be hunting those who crossed it.

Onyx came prepared. He hopped out of the truck, grabbing the wire cutters he brought with him. He snapped the barbed wire fence leading to the meadow. They kept their distance, still not knowing who was waiting on them.

Onyx drove the truck deeper into the meadow, focussing on the stone, when a face came into view. His stomach filled with sick dread when he realized who it was.

"Flip!" Ivy shouted before Onyx could. "That's Flip! We have to help him."

Ivy jumped out of the truck before Onyx slowed to a stop.

"Ivy wait!" Onyx called after her, but it was no use. She was already running across the meadow to Flip's stone likeness at the edge of the forest.

"If her undead warriors can't kill you, she'll turn you to stone before you cross? Is that it? You think you can hurt my friends? Think again!"

Ivy shouted into the forest. Onyx knew she was talking to Morgana, the Stone Witch. Ivy was pissed.

"You're not winning, you evil b-"

Ivy was cut off and blasted backward toward the fence. She struggled up, grimacing in pain. Onyx ran to her, helping her stand. He would worry about Flip later. They looked up for Morgana, but there was no sign of her, just her residual magic protecting the forest.

"Flip," Ivy sobbed.

Onyx looked Ivy over, brushing the dirt off her thin sweater and frayed jeans. As soon as she was on her feet, Ivy ran to the frozen statue and tried running her hands over it, like she had with Bud. She tried until she was exhausted, slumped over and panting.

"I can't," she turned to Onyx, teary-eyed.

"Can your mom? Your aunts?" Onyx asked.

Ivy wiped her tears and nodded.

"We just have to get him to the lodge."

Onyx tried to pick up the stone, but even for him, the guy who could bench press three hundred pounds, he couldn't get the stone statue to budge.

"Let me try," Ivy said.

She rubbed her hands together to warm them, then placed them on the stone. A slight hum filled the air, not audible, but a vibration you could feel. Ivy lifted the statue up, grimacing, and with a crushing thud, she set it down into the truck bed. Onyx just stood and stared. He didn't know what to make of it, so he started off a slow clap, causing Ivy to shoot him a glare.

"Who are you now? Harbor? Just get in the truck," she said with an eye roll.

Onyx complied.

Ivy pointed out the way to the lodge. It was about thirty minutes from town, outside of the boundary Ivy had placed around Big Cabin. When they pulled into the lodge, the door was already open. A silver haired woman in a deep cerulean robe paced in the driveway. As Onyx drove up, Ivy hopped out before he stopped the truck.

She really needs to quit doing that, Onyx thought to himself.

Together, Ivy and the woman floated the statue into the large cabin situated in front of the lake. He didn't know if he should follow. He was still mulling it over when a red haired girl in soccer shorts jogged to the truck.

"Hey, Onyx right? You can come in. My mom's working on him right now. What's his name?"

The girl talked so quickly that he had to stop a beat to process what she said.

"Yeah, um, his name's Flip, well, Fernando. We call him Flip because he freaks out about everything."

"Right," the girl motioned to the door. "Come with me."

Onyx followed who he assumed to be Ashley into the lodge. The high ceiling in the great room drew his attention upward, but he soon turned to another red haired woman who matched Ashley, along with Ivy and the silver haired woman from the driveway. They all had one hand on the statue version of Flip.

"Onyx," Ivy said, remembering that he hadn't ever met that part of her family. "This is my Aunt Cynthia, and my Aunt Megan."

"Ashley we need you," Megan said to the girl Onyx assumed to be her daughter. She then turned to him. "We're going to do all we can to reverse the petrification."

Onyx crossed muscular forearms in front of his chest, hoping they could change Flip back. He was their best wide receiver and they had play-offs coming up.

Ashley joined them, placing a hand on the statue along with her other family members. The statue made a slight cracking sound. Onyx wondered if Flip's bones were breaking. He got his answer when the stone finally cracked and gave way to a blinding light, turning Flip's outer stone shell to dust.

Onyx was amazed. He almost didn't see the other tall woman with shiny auburn hair appear on the balcony above the great room, but she was hard to miss. All of them were, but he guessed the one on the balcony was used to commanding attention.

"You'll have to burn the memories, Ashley," she murmured, uninterested, and then walked back into the darkness of the hallway.

Flip stood dazed in the center of the room. Cynthia told them it would take a minute for him to realize what happened, and in that time, Ashley could burn any memories away of him being turned to stone.

Cynthia and Megan left the room, ascending a wide staircase to the balcony, disappearing into the bedrooms.

Ivy took a nervous glance at Flip.

"It won't hurt him, will it?" Ivy asked her

cousin, as Ashley placed a hand on the side of Flip's head.

"You still don't trust me, do you?" Ashley asked, rolling her eyes. "I know what I'm doing."

CHAPTER 34

Something You Don't Know

Ivy clenched her teeth as Ashley moved a glowing red palm across Flip's face and across the right side of his head. Onyx wondered what angry words Ivy was holding back. He didn't have much time to think about it, because when Ashley finished up her magic, Flip jumped up and scanned the room for Onyx.

"Man!" he shouted. "That was some lit party, man. Thank you for inviting me. I honestly do appreciate it."

Ashley crossed her arms, admiring her handiwork. Flip spun around a few times in a break dance and then hopped up the side of Onyx's shoulder. He punched him in the shoulder a few times and then laughed, shaking one of Onyx's crossed arms.

"Ashley, you are the coolest. Always a pleasure, you know if you ever decide to throw another party please let me know, I was so glad to help you clean up. Looks like I did an excellent job," Flip literally patted himself on the back. "Onyx man, let's go. Let's not be rude, outstaying our welcome. These ladies have been so hospitable." Flip took Ashley's hand and kissed it, sending a blush across her cheeks. "You're a cutie. I'll be talking to you later after I win state. Maybe Onyx can help. I don't know. I'm the star though. Remember that, please."

Flip jogged out to the truck, with Onyx following him. Ivy paced behind Onyx, not knowing what to say to Ashley. Onyx could sense the tension. It was thick until Ashley broke the silence.

"You guys need to be careful. That witch in the forest is old and you're not as powerful as me, Ivy."

Oh, no she didn't, Onyx thought to himself. Girl, get ready for the Ivy bomb.

"Oh, really?" Ivy screeched. "You're not my mom. You don't get to tell me what to do."

Ashley stopped short.

"I'm not trying to tell you what to do. I'm just saying that we've never seen anything like this and you should watch what you're doing. I don't-"

"You don't what?" Ivy cut her off.

"Nothing," Ashley sighed. "It's just that when someone helps my friends, I usually say thank you, but whatever."

"Your friends," Ivy laughed. "You must have so many of them, Ashley."

Onyx could sense that this wasn't going to end well, so he walked around to the other side of the truck to start the engine.

"What's that supposed to mean?" Ashley shot back.

"So, you can burn memories, huh?" Ivy started. "If you can burn memories, why does the Alchemist's son still remember you? Huh? Why didn't you burn his memories?"

"How do you know that?" Ashley challenged, with an unmistakable edge to her voice. "That's my business. You don't even know what happened."

"I know that you think your crap smells like roses and you think you can boss me around," Ivy said.

"How do you know about Blaze?" Ashley demanded, her voice trembling. "Tell me!"

Ivy took a step back when she heard Onyx start the truck.

"So, there are some things even you don't know," Ivy said, slamming the door.

Her angry tears betrayed her as Onyx sped off. Onyx could see there was a rift between Ivy and her cousin. He could see she was hurting and unsure of herself. He could see she wouldn't be able to get right with Ashley until she felt okay. The frustrating thing was, he just didn't know how to help.

Chapter 35

The Descendants

Onyx looked at Ivy out of the corner of his eye on the way to her house. She knew what he was thinking. How could she be so mean to her own family? Ivy laughed a mirthless laugh to herself.

Ashley had everything going for her. She was the rarest witch. She banished a shadow phantom on her first try. She had two hot guys pining for her and she erased Flip's memory with a power Ivy had never seen or knew existed. How was she supposed to compete with that?

"You okay?" Onyx asked. He took her hand and kissed the top of her third knuckle. "I mean, apart from Flip being turned to stone and your lame cousin nagging at you."

"You don't think she's right?" Ivy asked.

"Hell no," Onyx said, then upped his voice an octave to make fun of Ashley. "You know Ivy, you should say thank you to me, Queen Ashley, for stooping to help you. I don't speak to commoners that much, but I'll make an exception. Also, I'm gonna need that gold star for actually doing the right thing."

Ivy laughed.

"You don't think I'm being a brat?"

"I always think you're being a brat, but she was rude to say that to you when you're just trying to help the town," Onyx said. "Besides, we have a lot to deal with and playing it safe isn't going to get us anywhere. She can take her water wings and go play in the kiddie pool. We have a stone witch to take out."

You're right, Ivy thought.

Her mom was waiting up for them when they pulled into her driveway. Cynthia had called. Camille wasn't mad. She made that clear, she just wanted to check and make sure Ivy was okay. Camille had some startling news of her own.

"I was at the ranger's station when Jay turned on the radio. Linc Phillips was found dead, stabbed through the chest at a lounge outside town. The Steel Club, have you ever heard of it?"

Ivy gasped.

"No, mom," Ivy shook her head. She had never heard of The Steel Club.

"Well, apparently, Linc is Price and Wade Phillip's brother and the project manager on the pipeline. They found him out by his car, stabbed through the chest. Stabbed all the way through, with what looked like a big sword."

"Like a Viking sword," Ivy concluded.

A look of sobering connection crossed her mother's face.

"We're going to have to get some rest and figure all this out in the morning. I talked to Jay and your father. We're meeting at eight at the ranger's station. Cynthia and Patricia are coming, too."

"So am I," Ivy insisted, but Camille shook her head.

"I need you to go to the lodge with Megan and Ashley. If anything happens," Camille trailed off.

Ivy agreed for the time being, but after she kissed her mom goodnight, she ran upstairs with a plan of her own.

If I can see Morgana create the boundary, Ivy thought, then maybe I can see her create the stone men.

Ivy grabbed a disc of quartz and stacked it on top of another disc of amethyst, sitting cross-legged on her bed. She sucked in a breath and stopped chewing on a tassel on her sweater, a nervous habit. The stones warmed and Ivy knew it was now or never.

"Show me Morgana," she said. "And the stone men."

The stones sputtered to life and crackled with electricity. Ivy thought they might produce a spark and set her covers on fire, but they didn't. Instead, they created a vacuum effect, sucking her down into the stones themselves. Ivy traveled through them in a vortex of pink and purple, landing on hard dirt. When she looked around, she was in the forest, but it looked different.

A river ran through the area that was now the dry creek bed. The meadow was more forest, with no end in sight. Ivy was trying to find her way through the trees when she heard the scream.

It was guttural and pained, but it was female.

Ivy ran toward the sound until figures came into view, human shadows. The warriors had turned to stone and Morgana was sitting in a pile of ashes. Ivy expected the stone warriors, but she didn't expect the blonde woman running to Morgana, followed by a boy, maybe fifteen.

"What did you do?" she screamed at Morgana. "Morgana, what did you do?"

Morgana looked up at the woman with pained eyes. She shook her head, blinded by tears. The woman examined the stone statues until she found the one she was looking for. With an inhuman wail, she sunk to her knees. The boy followed and wrapped his arms around her. They rocked together, one choking back tears and one wailing, in a dance of pure grief.

"I'm sorry," Morgana cried. "I'm sorry, I didn't know what I was doing. Syrine, please believe I didn't know what I was doing."

"You turned my husband, my son's father, to stone!" Syrine screeched.

Ivy almost couldn't process what happened next. Syrine produced a dagger from the folds of her dress. With wild eyes and shaking hands, she moved toward Morgana, who still had her head in her hands, crying.

After a few seconds of hesitation, Syrine grabbed Morgana's hair and sliced the blade across her throat. Morgana reached for her cut throat, blood seeping through her fingers and down her arms. She choked for a few seconds, staring at Syrine in disbelief, and then fell over, dead in the middle of Harek's ashes.

Ivy balked at the scene. She had never seen anything so gruesome or intense. So Morgana was really dead. She was murdered. Ivy was still lost in thought when she felt the air cool behind her. She turned around to face the image of Morgana she knew from the forest.

"Did you see what you came to see through the stones?"

Her voice was cold but held a whisper of hope. Ivy turned back to Morgana's body. Syrine and her son walked out of the forest as Morgana's body broke into a million tiny shards and disintegrated into the earth.

Ivy turned back to Morgana. She wasn't evil. She wasn't the enemy. She was lost and alone, scared and confused in her grief and in her magic. Ivy's guilt sank to the bottom of her stomach, sitting thick like tar. Maybe Ashley wasn't the enemy either. Maybe she was scared, like Morgana and hiding in her own forest.

"Is Onyx related to them?" Ivy asked.

Morgana nodded.

"After she killed me, Syrine took Alfie to a nearby tribe. They assimilated and married into the tribe. Alfie is Harek's nephew. So yes, your Onyx is related to my Harek."

"Is that why you haven't killed me, or turned me to stone?" Ivy asked.

Morgana smiled a mercurial upturn of her lips.

"We cannot kill our own kind."

Lucky me, Ivy's thoughts dripped with sarcasm.

"Why don't you just leave?"

Morgana shook her head.

"I cannot leave them behind. Their bodies must be turned to ash or they will never enter Valhalla."

Morgana pointed to the stone men crowded around her. Ivy understood. They were her only friends and had served the king loyally, still to this day. Ivy glanced back, noticing the small line on Morgana's neck. It was thinner than the marks on her face.

"I guess you didn't get all your scars at the same time," Ivy remarked.

"No one gets all their scars at one time, young witch," Morgana returned. "I will use the descendants to show you, but I will need your help."

She was beginning to fade. The whole forest was beginning to fade. Ivy felt sucked back into her bedroom. She hit the pillow with a force that sent her head smashing back into her headboard. The stones on her bed had cracked in two.

Ivy let out an unstoppable yawn and before she knew it, she had descended into a deep, exhausted, dreamless sleep.

CHAPTER 36

You Have To Know That

Ivy woke to her phone buzzing beside her. She hoped it would be Onyx. She couldn't wait to tell him what she found out. Morgana was dead. She was murdered by her friend who was a distant ancestor to Onyx. Ivy's head buzzed. Even though Morgana was dead, the stone men would be active until Morgana had moved on to the next life, but she couldn't leave the stone men behind. She was trapped on Earth in an endless cycle of pain, guilt, and confusion.

If witches can convert pain to power, Ivy mused, then Morgana has been growing stronger this whole time. Still, something nagged at her. Why was Morgana fading away? Was it her other cryptic message to Ivy? The Stone Witch's words dug into her side.

We are weakest before our hour of greatest strength.

Ivy saw Onyx's name on her phone and

picked it up. She immediately launched into her excited deluge of thoughts.

"She's dead, Onyx. I found out last night through a spell. She was murdered in the forest."

The line went silent. Ivy fumbled with her phone, thinking she may have dropped the call.

"Onyx?"

"I don't know how you can say that to me," he said through wracked sobs, "but I really hope that's a sick joke, Ivy. I really do, because-"

"Morgana," Ivy interrupted, trying to explain herself. "We've been trying to figure it out, and I saw Morgana. I saw her."

"Oh my God," Onyx broke down into heaving breaths.

"What?" Ivy asked, the alarm rising in her stomach. "What's wrong?"

"It's Bailey," Onyx stammered out. "She's gone. She wasn't in her bed this morning. She always comes and wakes me up to watch Charlie Brown Thanksgiving when we're out for break, but she didn't. So, I went looking for her and she's gone."

Ivy could hear the sobs tearing through his chest. She couldn't believe she said that about Morgana. Onyx must have had a heart attack.

"Did you look everywhere? All around the property?"

"Yes," Onyx gulped in air to fill his lungs, collapsed from panic. "I looked everywhere around our property, all her favorite hiding spots."

"Did your mom take her to your grandma's to help with Thanksgiving dinner?" Ivy asked, trying to think of everything.

"No," Onyx answered. "They had a big fight last night about her going to help. Mom said she was still too little. I've tried to call my mom and my dad. I'm scared to call the cops. I don't want anyone else killed with the stone men still attacking people. I don't know what to do, Ivy. Please help."

Ivy thought back to the time Beckett had lost her in the Superstition Mountains, about a month before he died. She remembered him crying and squeezing her almost to death when he found her, playing with an old doll left behind in one of the ghost towns. He said he walked around the same mountain ten times. He wasn't thinking clearly with the panic clouding him. Ivy and Beckett both had cried until their parents found them, clutching each other in the old general store. Ivy wished she had a stone to see, but she cracked both of them looking for Morgana last night.

"You'll find her," Ivy assured, then corrected herself. "We'll find her. She can't be far. We have to go to the lodge, and then we have to go back to the forest."

"No way," Onyx said, trying to sound braver than he felt. "I'm not letting you go back there. I'll go by myself."

"We have to do this together, Onyx," Ivy insisted, remembering Beckett, shoulders slumped in relief when he found her. "Remember, it takes two. Besides, I have to go. I have to. Beckett would have searched an entire mountain range for me."

"Okay," Onyx relented. "Okay. I'll pick you up in five."

The two of them were silent for the most part, driving to the lodge. Ivy knew what she had to do. She needed to grab one of the seeing stones from the large back den in the lodge where the family kept their artifacts, find Bailey, and go get her. Even though the lodge was thirty minutes away, it was the fastest thing she knew to do.

Silent tears still streamed down Onyx's face.

"I can't believe I'm crying in front of you," Onyx chuckled.

"Why?" Ivy asked, lacing her fingers with his.

"Because I'm a guy," he said through a pained breath.

"So?" Ivy replied, squeezing his hand. "You're a human and your sister is missing. I can't freaking believe I said what I said to you when you called."

"It was a misunderstanding," Onyx said with a wisdom beyond his sixteen years. "They happen. A lot. I hope this whole thing is just a misunderstanding, but I don't think it is."

They pulled into the drive in front of the lodge. Ashley was already out the door. She ran down the steps with the fluid strides of a gazelle, almost banging into the truck.

"I don't want to fight," Ashley said as Ivy stepped down from the truck. It was like she knew that both of them being together out in front of the lodge spelled trouble. Ivy surprised them both by wrapping her arms around Ashley. Ashley started to cry.

"I heard you coming," Ashley explained, shaking away her tears. "I've never heard you before, but I heard you coming."

"I know. I'm sorry," Ivy began, interrupting Ashley with gulps of air punctuating her own sobs. Ashley pulled Ivy in tighter. Ivy's own tears overwhelmed her as she told her cousin what she should have said months ago. "I'm sorry Ashley. I know you were scared. I know you're still scared. I'm scared of my own magic, too. I was so jealous of you because you got your first spell right, but I shouldn't have treated you like that. I'm sorry. I'm so sorry."

Ashley wiped her tears away, but more sprang out to fill their place.

"I didn't get it right," Ashley laughed. "I fainted after I did it. Dom had to carry me to Aunt Patricia's. I don't know how I can do some of the things I do. Sometimes, it just comes out and it's scary. It's so scary, and I'm afraid I'm going to hurt someone."

Just like her, Ivy thought. Just like Morgana.

"But we have to go," Ashley's insistence

broke through Ivy's epiphany. "We have to go find Bailey. Dom's here. He's going, too. We can't let you do this alone. Mom, Aunt Patricia, Aunt Cynthia, they all went with Aunt Camille to the ranger's station, but we can't just sit here."

Olivia came trotting out, but before she could get to them, Ashley buried her face in Ivy's shoulder.

"Dom would have gone through anything, he'd go anywhere to find Veya. He's a good guy, Ivy. I love him. I love Dom. I do," Ashley said, shaking and crying in Ivy's arms, wrapped up in Dom's Madrid hoodie.

"I know," Ivy assured her. "I know you do. And he loves you."

Olivia ran down the steps, following them. Olivia could read Ivy better than anyone, so when she stopped in front of Onyx's truck, she already knew what she'd need.

"I can't find any of the stones," Olivia said, panting. "You think you can use the cliffside? Or the red clay? I read that stone witches can see through it. It'll be murky, but I think you can do it."

Dom followed Olivia, nodding to Ivy and clasping Onyx's hand for a handshake. Seeing that Onyx was close to inconsolable, Dom wrapped his arm around Onyx's shoulder. Onyx choked out another sob, before collecting himself.

"You're alright, man," Dom assured him. "You're good. We're gonna find your sister."

Ivy, overcome with empathetic hurt for Onyx, closed her eyes, placing them against her palms. Olivia and Ashley wrapped their arms around her. As they did, a vision flashed through her head. Bailey was playing with sticks on a leafy carpet, shaded by trees, surrounded by the crags and boulders she knew so well. It was like Ivy saw through her own bones what Morgana was seeing in the present.

"I don't need the stones," Ivy said, looking at her family with piercing certainty. "I know where she is."

"I know you do," Onyx took Ivy's hand with a trust that was almost devastating.

Ivy met his gray eyes, marked with flecks of black like the face of the Stone Witch.

"Let's go get our girl."

CHAPTER 37

So We Meet Again

They stood at the edge of the forest. Ivy, Onyx, Ashley, Dom, and Olivia clasped hands and readied themselves for Ivy's spell that would allow them to travel into the forest and escape Morgana's petrification.

"I can't," Ivy turned to Ashley. "I can't. You do it. You're more powerful than I am."

Ashley sucked in a breath, and forming a pained smile, she shook her head.

"Not here, I'm not," Ashley grasped her cousin's hand. "You've got this. I know you've got this."

Ivy knelt and placed a palm to the earth. At once, she envisioned Morgana and Harek, crumbling a mountainside, defeating a rival army together, powered by not only their love, but their friendship, and their respect for each other. The crimson ribbon glowed in Ashley's hand, waiting to be extended.

"Onyx," Ivy turned to look up at his set jaw

and determined eyes. "We're going to have to do this together."

"Anything for you," was his immediate reply, and Ivy knew he meant it.

Ivy stretched her palm out to the forest, as Morgana had done hundreds of years ago. Onyx instinctively placed his palm over hers. When he did, a line of crimson light streamed around their hands, and then out into the forest.

Olivia took a step back and looked at Ashley. They were both awestruck as a thin barrier, domed over the land, almost like glass, vibrated and then crackled across its surface. A thin, high pitch pierced the forest. Olivia covered her ears and Dom wrapped his arms around Ashley, muffling the noise with his hoodie.

The light blazed from their hands for a few more blinding seconds, and then the barrier disintegrated, falling like tiny snowflakes around the land.

Ivy was still standing.

"Let's test it," Olivia said, breaking the silence.

She moved to cross into the forest, but Dom held her back.

"I'll go."

Dom didn't waist any time jogging into the forest. Ivy could feel Ashley's love for him rolling off in waves, but there was something else there. Ivy couldn't tell, and the feeling was gone as quickly as it had hit her. Ivy glanced at Olivia. Her green eyes were glowing.

"Ivy, come on," Onyx called.

Ivy snapped out of her trance, and followed him into the forest. When they reached the river bed, they saw them through the trees. Onyx and Dom ran through the woods, hopping over small boulders in their way.

Morgana had called all the stone men back, and they stood, surrounding her and a small shape that Ivy recognized as Bailey. Bailey held a small bird in the her lap. The bird had a long beak and legs, and white feathers tipped with gray. Its eyes shone grass green in the sunlight that streamed through, forming a small circle on the forest floor.

"Bailey!"

Onyx ran to her, but she didn't get up to move. Onyx stopped short in front of the Stone Witch.

"Let me have my sister," Onyx commanded. "I swear if you hurt her-"

"You will find your sister unharmed," Morgana assured.

"Wait," Olivia interrupted.

Olivia produced her phone from her pocket. She clicked the camera open and snapped a picture of Bailey and the bird she held. Bailey nodded. She set the bird on the ground, gently, and then ran to Onyx.

The sweet scene tore at Ivy's heart,

reminding her of Beckett. Ashley wrapped her arms around Dom as he choked back a small sob.

Ivy turned to Morgana, grasping her hand, slightly outstretched. Her hand felt cool and small in Ivy's.

"I am ready," Morgana confessed. "It has been so long since I have seen him."

"Ashley?"

Her cousin heard her thoughts. Ashley saw what she needed to do and before Ivy could say anything more, Ashley produced a flame from her hand. Then together, Ivy reverted the stone warriors to a lighter, petrified ash, allowing Ashley to ignite them. The stone men burned, as they should have upon their deaths, the smoke from the pyres carrying their spirits to Valhalla. Morgana inhaled a sigh. The smoke washed over her face, taking the ash in her skin away.

"It takes two," Morgana smiled.

Soon, with Ivy and Ashley working together, Morgana looked on as all the stone men were set ablaze, a dozen spectacular funeral pyres fit for Viking warriors. One last stone man remained.

"I got this," Ivy told Ashley.

Ashley grabbed her cousin, pulling her close and kissing her cheek.

"I know you do," Ashley whispered. "I love you."

"I love you, too," Ivy told her.

Ivy then placed a palm on the last stone

statue. The stone man hummed with life as the stone cracked away, revealing the man beneath the layer of rock.

"Arin," Morgana gasped.

The sky shook with thunder as Arin, Harek's brother, strode to Morgana. He extended a hand, just as he had done the two times he brought her ashore.

"My queen, I am charged with bringing you home."

The clouds parted and streamed down, forming a stairway to an opening, framed by sunlight. Morgana had avoided the sunlight for so long.

Harek stood in the doorway, along with Father Thomas and Syrine, waiting for Morgana, calling her home. Arin grasped her hand, but Morgana turned back to Ivy.

"If all is forgiven, I can go."

Ivy smiled. She brought her hands to her face to wipe away the tears. Morgana had forgiven Syrine, Ivy and Ashley had forgiven each other, and most of all, Ivy forgave herself.

"Yes," Ivy said, feeling Onyx wrap his arm around her. "All is forgiven."

Morgana, her face no longer marked, gave Ivy just a hint of a smile before taking Arin's hand and ascending the steps to Harek. Whether he was in Heaven or Valhalla, Ivy couldn't say. Perhaps they were the same place. Perhaps it was all just love and light and the ones you care about the most at that point.

    The sunlight was blinding. Ivy couldn't see Morgana make it to the top, but she was sure she made it, back home, back to Harek where she belonged.

CHAPTER 38

The Salt Crane

They heard the four wheelers roaring into the forest before they saw them. Camille and the rest of her sisters were calm, but Jay Rainwater was frantic. He jumped off the all-terrain vehicle practically before it stopped.

"Bailey Jade!" Jay bellowed in to the clearing. "Onyx, what happened?"

Onyx hadn't told anyone except Ivy that his sister was missing. In his adrenaline fueled panic, he hadn't even left voicemails for his parents. Still, Jay saw the smoke from the trees and when he drove into the forest, twelve flaming piles of ash surrounded his children. It was enough to make any father have a heart attack.

Onyx gave his dad a blank stare.

"Well?" his dad shouted. "Start talking!"

"It was a lightning strike," Ivy interrupted, answering for him. "It came out of nowhere."

"Twelve times in the same place?" Jay asked, incredulous at the phenomena.

"No," Ivy answered, recalling the explanation she was given on the most painful day of her life. "It just struck one of the statues. It branched out to the others."

Ivy remembered the day Beckett was killed. Lightning struck him and then branched out, hitting his friends, but Beckett was the only one who didn't survive.

"It can happen," Camille confirmed.

"Wow," Jay scratched his head. "I'm just glad you're all okay."

"More than okay," Olivia piped up from the back.

As the fires began to die, Olivia led everyone to a tree a few paces away. In a small, hollowed out portion of the trunk, the strange bird rested on a pile of green and gray speckled eggs.

"Is that?" Jay gasped, and cocked his head to the side, not believing what he was seeing. "Is that the salt crane?"

Jay peered into the tree, past the rough-hewn bark to the small, strange bird perched on top of the eggs. He grabbed his camera and snapped a few pictures, not wanting to disturb the bird.

Jay radioed the station and told the other rangers to call the Wildlife Federation. They had finally found the endangered species that would push the pipeline out of the park.

Olivia produced a paper from her pocket and handed it to her mom with a guilty shrug.

"I took this from your office," she admitted.

It was a poem from the late poet, Angelina Fontanez.

The Salt Crane

Lines drawn in earth and sand,
Cutting deep across the land.
Emerald eyes and silver wings,
The Salt Crane alludes to greater things.

She stays hidden in the forest folds.
Only the lost know what secret she holds.
The promised one follows this keeper of the skies,
The descendants must only find where she lies.

Helen read the poem aloud, sending chills down Ivy's body. Olivia must have known what the bird was the minute she saw it.

"I'll radio this in," Jay said. "Onyx." He motioned for his son to follow.

"You got Bay?" Onyx asked Ivy.

"Yeah," Ivy said, wrapping an arm around Bailey's shoulder. "We're going bra shopping."

When everyone was back at the ranger's station, Onyx passed around blankets and hot cocoa. They called Tiffany to tell her what had happened. Well, Jay's version of what had happened. She was relieved that no one was hurt and insisted that everyone make their way to Grandma

Rainwater's house for Thanksgiving dinner. Cynthia warmly accepted on all their behalf.

Olivia moved to sit by Ivy and Ashley, wrapped up in the same blanket. Ashley sipped a steaming cup of herbal tea while Ivy stared into space.

"What does it mean?" Ivy asked. "The poem? The promised one?"

Olivia knew Ivy was going to ask. Some people can just read a poem and accept it at face value, but some read into it a little more. Olivia had been studying her mother's favorite poet and was convinced that her poems were more than just pretty words. She had also been studying her Grandma Cynthia's documents and making connections between the two.

"According to some of the documents from The Light, there will be another Luminosa after the omen appears. I think that omen is the salt crane."

"The Luminosa, like the most powerful witch?" Ivy asked. She had heard the Healer in Paris talk about the Luminosa. They used to be plentiful, but now they were very rare. No one had seen a Luminosa in hundreds of years. They're like phantoms.

"Yes, but a phantom with all the powers of the elements," Olivia explained. "Could you imagine? Our powers are limited. I guess it's nature's way of telling us to watch it, that we aren't immortal, but a Luminosa has every elemental power. They're born that way."

"Wow," Ashley furrowed her brows. "You think?"

"I don't know," Olivia admitted. "But Morgana is gone. And her power had to go somewhere."

"Not to any of us," Ivy looked around at her cousins. "We would know it already."

"Not to any of us," Olivia echoed, but then directed a very pointed look at Onyx's little sister, drawing on a notepad at her dad's desk. "But we weren't alone in that forest."

"No," Ivy drew out the word, disbelieving, and crossed her arms. "You think?"

"I don't know," Olivia shrugged. "I can't see it. Nothing has been decided. I guess, only time will tell."

CHAPTER 39

Hashtag Blessed

Jay Rainwater came jogging through his childhood home with a fist raised in victory.

"We did it!" he shouted into the small, clapboard house.

The living room was filled with football-loving guys, young and old. They erupted into cheers normally reserved for a touchdown. Onyx stood up off the sinking, floral couch and wrapped his arms around his dad.

"I knew it, Dad. What did they say?" he asked, with a wide grin, full of expectation.

"Well," Jay began, "the Wildlife Federation decided that the pipeline had to be rerouted since the crane is an endangered species. They're sending a team out on Monday to research and collect some data. The pipeline has to stay out of the park entirely. There's no way that Phillips Oil is digging up one more crumb of dirt on Big Cabin Nature Reserve and National Park."

Onyx pumped his fist. Ivy and Olivia were

in the kitchen making deviled eggs. When she heard the news, Olivia stepped her way into the living room with the platter in hand. She handed the platter of eggs to Harbor and Onyx, who downed three each within a minute.

"Excuse me, Mr. Rainwater," Olivia interjected, her brows knitted together in confusion. "How did Phillips Oil even manage to get the original approval to build a pipeline through a part of the park anyhow?"

Jay shook his head. "Just one of the grand things about politics. Some lobbyist convinced the environmental committee to vote on granting Phillips Oil an exception. The thing is, when they approved the construction, they were using an altered map. One of the engineers on the project altered the map so it looked as though they were going just on the outer border, when in reality, they were cutting through the interior part of the park. According to the plans, they were planning on clearing a good part of that forest, too."

"That's awful," Ivy winced.

"I know," Jay said. "And you'll never believe who the lobbyist and engineer were."

Onyx, Ivy, and Olivia leaned in. Harbor grabbed two more eggs. Dom and Ashley joined the conversation, followed by Brooklynn Peters, Ashley's best friend, down for a visit at the lodge. Brooklynn had helped Ashley defeat the shadow phantom last year at the Phillips Museum in downtown Tulsa, and was no stranger to the Phillips family legacy.

"Who?" Ashley asked.

"Julie Carr. You may know her as Julie Carr-Phillips, Price Phillips' wife, and Scott Roy."

"Caleb's dad?" Onyx asked in disbelief.

"I know," Jay said, shaking his head, "but the guy is genius and a brain like that doesn't come cheap. I'm sure Wade and Price are making sure he's handsomely compensated. Anyhow, they're both under investigation. The police have even named them as persons of interest in Linc's murder investigation. I don't know what's going to happen."

Ivy was going to ask about Caleb when Onyx's grandma interrupted them with the dinner bell. Ivy smiled. She actually had an old tin dinner bell.

Everyone gathered around and filled their plates with roasted turkey, venison, cornbread dressing, mashed potatoes, sweet potato casserole, squash, and green beans. Harbor and Onyx were already chewing on buttered dinner rolls between loading their plates with food. Bailey darted in and out, filling her plate with mostly potatoes and feeding bites of turkey to Pickle, Ashley's tiny Pomsky puppy.

Even though they had polished off a tray of stuffed mushrooms and jalapeño poppers, Onyx, Harbor, and Dom were shifting in their seats, waiting for the girls to sit down so they could start eating round two. The kids were all gathered around a table in the backyard when a familiar face popped in.

"I didn't think you'd make it!" Harbor jumped up, extending his hand to Dylan, his friend from Prue that Ivy recognized as the grumpy, but good looking catcher from the baseball game.

"Hey man, glad you could come," Onyx grasped Dylan's hand in a firm handshake.

Brooklynn pushed her blonde hair back behind her ears. A flush spread over her cheeks.

"I'm gonna go get some food and talk at ya in a bit," Dylan nodded with a slight smile.

"Cheese and sprinkles," Brooklynn said as soon as he left. She held up her spoon to check her hair, then swiped some cherry gloss across her lips.

Ivy had to laugh on the inside. So, she wasn't alone! Even Ashley's all-state soccer star, butt-kicking best friend gets wobbly in the knees when a cute ex-boyfriend stops by. Still, Ivy concluded, Dylan didn't seem like he wanted the "ex" in the title. Maybe that's why he's so cantankerous, Ivy mused. That, or he's related to Bud.

Ivy finished with her turkey, so she clicked open Instagram while waiting for Onyx to finish the mountain of food on his plate. She stopped on one of Trystan's photos. The caption made her smile.

"Hanging with Madison on Thanksgiving. I love the shirt she bought for me to wear so I could match her dress, and I even got some tofu turkey for her. #veggiegirlfriend #matchymatchy #blessed"

Ivy smiled. There's somebody for everybody, she thought. When she saw that Onyx was finished with his plate, she went into habit mode. Onyx always wanted dessert.

"You want some pie?" she asked.

"No thanks. I think I'm full," Onyx answered.

"You're what?" the whole table asked in unison.

Onyx even surprised himself. He laughed a little delirious chuckle.

"I'm full," he announced, and went off to take a nap in his grandma's oldest recliner. He slept comfortably and soundly, better than he had in years. A few minutes later, Ivy went to check on him, snoring lightly through his turkey coma.

"I'm thankful for you, Onyx Rainwater," she whispered, thinking about everything they had overcome together these past few months. Ivy was a new person. Gone were the fears and insecurities. She had forgiven the past, and forgiven herself. "You gave me back myself. You changed my life, even though I thought it was carved in stone."

CHAPTER 40

SIDE BY SIDE

Across the state, at a small cemetery in Tulsa, resting inconspicuously close to the Phillips Museum, a small party gathered at a graveside. A man in plainclothes, escorted by a correctional officer from the David L. Moss Criminal Justice Center, sat away from the family. Lincoln Phillips was being laid to rest. He was survived by his two brothers, Price and Wade Phillips. He had no wife or children.

After his casket was lowered, Scott Roy spoke in a low voice to Wade Phillips while tears fell from Julie Carr-Phillips' eyes. Price's wife had always been fond of his little brother Linc. Two teens in black stood side by side.

The boy, tall and thin, in a black suit and slim, black tie turned to the girl with icy blonde locks, clad in a sleek black sheath dress. Her spiked heels sunk a bit into the cold, damp earth.

"Are you okay?" he asked her, taking her

hand, lightly, feeling the feather weight of her slim, manicured fingers.

"No, not really," Kylie Phillips answered. "Your dad and my stepmom are suspects in my uncle's murder investigation and those witches are still walking free. I know this was all their fault. Three people are dead because of them. We'll be okay, though. We always have been."

Price's daughter glanced to her stepmother. Her brother, home from Dartmouth, stood next to Julie Carr-Phillips, talking in a low voice. Kylie sighed. She toyed with the ring on Caleb's finger, tracing the symbol, a circle with a slash through the center. He hardly ever wore it.

At this very moment, Price's friends on the outside were collecting pieces of concrete from their broken pipeline, now tainted with stone magic. The samples were bound for the lab.

"Where are we going?" Caleb asked, his cheeks made ruddy by the biting wind.

"You'll see," Kylie teased. "Somewhere they can't get to us. I have missed you, though."

Kylie wanted to wrap her slim arms around Caleb, but she resisted.

"I've missed you too, Kylie," Caleb whispered. "There's no one like you. I promise you. Those witches are not going to get the best of us."

"I'm not stopping until every single one of them is dead," Kylie spat.

"Not before we extract their magic," Caleb

reminded her. "They're only human, flesh and blood like you and me."

Kylie rested her head on Caleb's shoulder. Tiny flakes of snow began to float down. Caleb brushed them off Kylie's sleek hair.

Kylie turned to her cousin, sitting in the front row with the other mourners.

"Are you still on your phone, Sadie Lee?"

Sadie Lee rolled her eyes at Kylie.

"That's not real, Kylie," Sadie Lee whined. "You're making stuff up to scare me again, like you used to when we were little."

"Oh, it is real," Kylie snapped. "When Caleb and his dad extract the secret to those little skanks' magic. You'll see. Everyone will see. And then everyone will be on our side, getting rid of them forever."

CHAPTER 41

Are You Sure?

The surface of the small creek shimmered. The water rose, forming a solid, human form. When the water stilled and fell away, Cynthia Stiles was left standing at the edge of the forest on Big Cabin Nature Reserve. She lit a single match that flamed up as tall as a roaring bonfire. When the flames died down and the smoke cleared, Patricia Freya stood next to her sister.

Camille Jasper's shorter frame appeared, silhouetted on the side of a boulder. As she stepped out of the boulder, her skin turned from a dark gray to a pale peach. A single leaf fell from one of the tall trees at the edge of the forest. As it fell, Megan Nirran's slim, athletic body appeared, standing next to Camille.

"Are you sure?" Patricia asked.

Camille gestured to the sign, her features remaining grim. Patricia swallowed hard. Her sisters could practically hear her heart hammering in her chest. She paced across the grass to touch the letters on the sign in the abandoned construction site.

"Barlow Pipe and Supply," she breathed. "A subsidiary of Barlow Industries, well I'll be damned."

Patricia's chest seized recalling her last memories of Kenneth Barlow, twenty years ago. A modern office on the top floor of the tallest building downtown, his lips on hers, a smashed highball glass, and a river of tears. Patricia stared at the metal sign bearing her ex-fiance's name and company until the sheet of metal crumpled like a piece of notebook paper.

"Kenneth Barlow," Patricia began, crossing her arms, "can go straight to hell."

"I'm sure he'll get there soon enough," Cynthia quipped, "but regardless, we need Louisa to come home. We've all seen it. The Alchemists are growing and getting stronger. They learn more about us with each passing day. For all we know, Barlow could have sold us out to them."

Kenneth Barlow owned Barlow Industries, a chemical and mechanical research facility. The facility produced new products, everything from light bulbs to weapons for the United States Army. He was quite a success story, considering that fifteen years ago, he was selling guns illegally. He had gotten Louisa's husband, Derrick Vesper involved with the murder of an illegal arms dealer. Derrick was convicted and sent to prison for thirty years while Kenneth walked free.

"That seems like something he would do," Patricia admitted, her disgust seeping through.

"Well, I'm not calling Louisa," Megan insisted, crossing her arms in front of her chest.

Cynthia shot her a look and then clicked open her cell phone. It rang on speaker three times, then Louisa Vesper picked up. Cynthia was at a bit of a loss since she expected it to go to voicemail. After a few beats of silence, Louisa's voice snapped through the phone.

"What do you want?" Louisa asked.

"We need you to come home," Cynthia said, as if trying to ease a tiger out of its lair. "We need you to bring Ariel and come home. The Alchemists are back. Kenneth Barlow is in business with Price and Wade Phillips and their youngest brother, Lincoln, is dead. We need you to come home."

"I don't care if Kenneth Barlow and Price Phillips get married, I'm not coming back," Louisa stood obstinate. "No way, no how."

"You know Price is in prison, right?" Patricia interrupted. "At David L. Moss, with Derrick."

She let the line hang silent.

"Derrick can take care of himself," Louisa said, a bitter taste clouding her mouth. "He made his choice. I'm staying here, and so is Ariel."

The four sisters fell silent as the line went dead. They heard what she said, but they all knew, Louisa would be back, and she would be bringing Derrick Vesper's daughter with her.

CHAPTER 42

CHECKMATE

Onyx stood up and shook the kid's hand across the chessboard. He had beaten another opponent in the semi-finals and was on his way to the final match of the state chess tournament in Tulsa. The football team had won the state championship a week after Thanksgiving. Onyx was excited, but watching from the stands, Ivy had never seen Onyx happier than at this moment.

She looked at the logo on Watson Academy's gym floor. The Watson Vikings. Ivy laughed to herself. She wondered about Morgana and Harek from time to time. Part of her knew that Morgana was where she belonged and that she could finally let go of the land she had clung to for so long. Besides, Ivy had the best part of Harek standing down on the Vikings seal adorning Watson's gym floor.

"Dang," Isaac Aalish smiled as he shook Onyx's hand. "Not bad, not bad."

"That's okay, Isaac. You did a great job," Brooklynn congratulated him.

Brooklynn, Ashley, and Dom came to watch their friend and Brooklynn's teammate from Tech Team at Watson Academy. The final match was only fifteen minutes away. Nervous energy fluttered in Ivy's stomach.

"You okay?" Ivy asked, bringing him a Dr. Pepper and quick kiss.

"Yeah," Onyx smiled. "I have Dr. Pepper and you. The park is safe and I'm in a state championship for the second time. What more do I need?"

Ivy could tell he was relaxed and happy. The past month had been smooth sailing, just as it should have been. Still, something nagged at her. The year had been a rocky one and she seemed to always be the one throwing the stones.

"It was always me, wasn't it?" Ivy asked. "It was always me, messing things up with you."

"Well, yeah," Onyx laughed.

"I knew it," Ivy groaned.

She buried her face in his shoulder. Onyx dug her out of his side and cupped her face in his hands.

"You pick the best times," he said, rubbing his nose on hers. "But let me tell you this. Ivy wasn't messing things up with me, Ivy was messing things up with her true self. You weren't being you, not the real you. When you finally decided to let it go, and trust both you and me, we couldn't mess it up, not even if we tried."

Ivy tilted her head. Onyx was pretty smart.

"So, we're like destined to be together? All the stars align?"

"Yep," Onyx said, planting a quick but sure kiss on her forehead. "Checkmate." .

Jennifer Campbell is the author of the Phantom Elements series. She was a school librarian and developed the series after being asked for the spooky books at least twice per day. She hopes these books will be spooky enough. Jennifer currently lives in Tulsa, Oklahoma, with her husband and son.

Stay Connected

Want more Phantom Elements in your mailbox? Just send an email to:
 jennifercampbell@chromastorybooks.com
with the subject line "sign me up."

You'll recieve Phantom Updates, free printables, extras, and information on all things Phantom Elements. And no spam. Ever.

Follow our Phantom Elements Facebook page for updates from Jennifer and all things Phantom!

Acknowledgements

As always, I need to send a bottomless amount of love and thanks to my family. I couldn't have done any of this bookish fun without the love and support of my husband, Micah. He's always my biggest fan. Thanks to my son, Noah, who always waited on me to "just finish this chapter" before we could go to the pool.

To my parents and editors, Alan and Peggy Hulsey, thank you for putting up with me for thirty four years and hopefully longer. They checked my homework and now they check my books. Not all heroes wear capes.

Thank you to the indie author community, especially I.A.S. for all your knowledge, support, friendship, and crazy fun.

Finally, and most importantly, thank you to Our Heavenly Father who has blessed me beyond measure and allowed me to share my stories with His world. I do not deserve Your grace, but I receive it anyhow and I am eternally grateful.

Family is everything.
Love always, Jennifer.

Made in the USA
Coppell, TX
26 February 2021